Wellington and Boot

Humphrey Carpenter
and
Jenny McDade

MACMILLAN
CHILDREN'S BOOKS

First published 1991 by Macmillan Children's Books

Piper edition published 1993 by Pan Macmillan Children's Books
This edition reprinted 1995 by Macmillan Children's Books
a division of Macmillan Publishers Limited
Cavaye Place London SW10 9PG
and Basingstoke

Associated companies throughout the world

ISBN 0 330 32274 5

3 5 7 9 8 6 4

A CIP catalogue record for this book is available from
the British Library

Printed and bound in Great Britain by
Cox & Wyman Ltd, Reading, Berkshire

1

Welcome to
Wonderful Wibberley

"What sort of place is Wibberley-on-the-Wold?" Keith Murray asked his mum and dad. They were eating a scrappy lunch of crisps and KitKats, sitting on the dirty grass beside a main road, along which lorries were thundering. A sign near them said, "London 92, Wibberley 11".

"I've told you before, Keith," said his mum. "It's a nice little country town, isn't it, Dad?"

Keith's dad, Morris Murray, who had a face like a sick spaniel, nodded glumly.

"But has it got a football team?" asked Keith. "What's my new school like? Is it near our house, so I can bring friends home to tea?"

His mum, Muriel Murray, was more interested in the ladder that had just appeared in her last pair of tights than in Keith's endless questions. "Don't ask me," she snapped. "I've never even seen the place." She shot Keith's dad a coolish glance. "Ask *him*. *He* bought it from an advert."

Until a week ago, Morris Murray had kept a corner sweet and tobacconist shop in a London suburb. But it had never done well. People who came in looking for something tended to be put off by the gloomy sight of Morris behind the counter. Most of them went away without buying anything. So the shop had failed to make enough money, and finally Morris announced that there was no choice but to sell up and move away. They'd decided to go to the country, stuck a pin in a map, and discovered Wibberley-on-the-Wold.

"Is Dad going to open another shop there?" asked Keith, as he and his mum chucked their picnic rubbish in a bin – though there didn't seem much point in doing this, because the grass was littered with other people's rubbish.

"You know perfectly well he's not," snapped his mum. "Just look at him now. He's counting them again."

Morris had opened the back of the family's rusting Austin Maxi, and was peering into some cardboard boxes piled high inside. They were labelled "Golightly's Garden Gnomes".

"D'you really think anyone'll buy 'em, Mum?" whispered Keith. His mum didn't answer.

Twenty minutes later the family was driving past a signpost that said "Welcome to wonderful Wibberley-on-the-Wold. Be sure to visit the exclusive new developments by *Crawleyhomes*".

"Nearly there now, everyone," said Keith's dad, peering anxiously over his steering wheel.

"Thought you said it was a nice little country town, Morris," said Keith's mum.

"Doesn't look much like country to me, Dad," said Keith. "In fact it looks more like— "

2

"Rows and rows of building sites," said his mum acidly, as they rattled past signboard after signboard:

CRAWLEYHOMES
present
Exciting New Homes
at Prices *You* can Afford

VISIT OUR EXECUTIVE-STYLE SHOWHOME
Open Seven Days a Week
Free Satellite TV Dish with Every Purchase

CRAWLEYHOMES LUXURY ONE-BED MAISONETTES
Compact Residences for the First-Time Buyer
Only 256 left!

"But I was expecting thatched roofs and duck ponds," wailed Keith's mum. "Not row after row of these horrible little boxes. And who are these Crawleyhomes people? They seem to own everything round here."

"Don't worry, Mum," said Keith. "I'm sure our house'll be better. We won't have to live in one of these, will we, Dad?"

The rust-heap which was the Austin Maxi turned left, and left again, and drew up outside a very small house. There were piles of sand and other builders' leftovers, which looked as if they had been lying around for some time.

"What are you stopping here for, Morris?" said Keith's mum. "We're looking for Cherrytree Close."

"This is it," muttered Morris. And he pointed to yet another sign:

3

CHERRYTREE CLOSE
Another Charming Creation by
CRAWLEYHOMES
Distinctive Dwellings for the Smaller Family
PRICES SLASHED!

"Number seventeen, that's ours," said Morris, trying to sound proud.

"But it's *tiny*, Dad," said Keith. "It's even smaller than the others in the street. And *they're* small enough, aren't they, Mum?"

Muriel Murray's eyes had glazed over and she had gone a strange colour. She looked as if she was about to faint.

"It is somewhat compact, I grant you," said Morris.

"*Compact*?" screamed Muriel, suddenly regaining the power of speech. "This isn't a house, you fool, it's a HUTCH!"

Morris sighed. "I know you were expecting a cottage, love, hollyhocks in the garden and roses round the door, but they're too pricey. Anyhow, everywhere's like this these days. It's progress, you see. Gotta move with the times. Mind you," he continued, "it is a bit smaller than it looked in the advert." The family climbed out and stood amidst broken-open bags of cement.

"Small?" screamed Keith's mum. "It's hardly big enough for – for *pygmies*!"

"We got it cheap," said Morris lamely.

"Are you surprised?" fumed Muriel. "They ought to pay us to live in this. I bet they couldn't *give* it away to anyone except you. What have you brought us to, Morris?" she wailed.

4

"I mean, look at it, Dad," said Keith. "The ground floor's all garage."

"Come in handy for storing my gnomes, that will," said his dad.

"Drat your stupid gnomes," screamed Muriel. "What about my dancing school?" Many years earlier, before Keith was born, Muriel Murray had earned some money by giving dancing classes. She had been looking forward to starting again, in their new house, now that Keith was older and off her hands. "I can't hold classes here," she cried. "It's far too small."

"Hire a hall, then," muttered Morris.

"Hire a hall?" she snapped icily. "With what? We've hardly a penny left, after this move, to *eat* with, let alone hire halls."

"Now, dear," said Morris, "you'll soon be in your element, when you're ensconced in your new kitchen."

"And what am I supposed to cook in it?" Looking round at the rows of empty, unsold houses, she added "Anyway, I don't see any shops round here."

"It's not like London," said Morris. "There are no corner shops here, we'll have to find a supermarket."

2

The Du Maurier
School of Dancing

Several streets from Cherrytree Close, a white Rolls-Royce with the number-plate JCB 1 drew up outside a building. A big notice said:

CRAWLEYHAVEN
A CRAWLEYHOMES Development of Private
Apartments for the Elderly
Come to Wibberley and Grow Old on the Wold
£50,000 Deposit and You Can End Your Days in
a CRAWLEYHOME

Beneath, someone had hung a sign that said "Opening ceremony today".

J.C.B. Crawley, the multi-millionaire owner of Crawleyhomes, parked the white Rolls. In the back sat his wife Cherie, who had once been Miss Lovely Legs, and his daughter Krystle, who had just been thrown out of her eleventh very expensive boarding school that morning.

"What's this place, then, Dad?" asked Krystle as

she climbed out of the Rolls, chewing bubble-gum. "Cheapo rabbit-warren for the old crocks?"

"Leave it out, Princess," said J.C.B. Crawley, who looked more like the pop group manager he used to be, than a property millionaire. "This is real prestige development, all tastefully landscaped, see?" He pointed to a few withered-looking small trees, which had been hastily stuck into some heaps of earth and gravel. The effect might have been better if someone hadn't left a supermarket trolley lying on its side in front of them.

J.C.B. kicked the trolley aside as he and Cherie went to greet the Lady Mayor of Wibberley-on-the-Wold, Councillor Mrs Queenie Scroggs, who was waiting to join in the opening ceremony.

They all posed for the photographer from the *Woldshire Chronicle*, J.C.B. in his expensive leather overcoat, Cherie smiling trimly, as she had been taught when training to be a fashion model, and Councillor Mrs Scroggs wearing a hat decorated with artificial fruit. The picture might have come out quite well, but Krystle managed to get into it without anyone noticing, and made a rude face from the back.

After Councillor Queenie Scroggs had cut the tape and officially opened the flats, Cherie presented the first couple who had bought one with a Crawleyhomes gift token for a free Jacuzzi.

"What's a Jacuzzi?" the old people asked Mrs Scroggs.

"Isn't it one of them Japanese ornamental tree things?" she answered.

The three Crawleys, breathing sighs of relief, clambered into the Rolls and departed.

7

"Thought we'd pick up a few steaks from the supermarket on our way home, doll," said J.C.B. to Cherie as she powdered her nose. "Reckoned we could pretend we was an ordinary family for once," he added. "So I give all the servants the night off, like, so we three can have a real slap-up supper in the kitchen, see?"

"Mum doesn't know where the kitchen is," said Krystle.

"And I can't possibly cook, Jay," whined Cherie. "Not with my nails."

Meanwhile the Murray family had found the supermarket. A sign outside said:

CRAWLEYFOODS
HYPERMARKET for the HOME FREEZER

"Car park looks a bit full, dear, so I'll just turn the Maxi round while you're shopping," said Morris, who was trying to be nice to Muriel because of the house.

Muriel said nothing, but slammed the car door as she got out, causing a cloud of rust. Keith followed her into the supermarket, where they headed for canned foods. Muriel reckoned they could afford a tin of baked beans – but on the way they stopped at frozen meats. "We might just have enough for some mince," she said to Keith.

While Muriel debated the possibility of meat for dinner, the white Rolls-Royce with the number-plate JCB 1 drew into the supermarket car park. Cherie and Krystle got out, but J.C.B. sat at the wheel and lit a cigar.

"Aren't you coming in, Dad?" asked Krystle.

"Nah," said J.C.B., who was already getting bored with his "ordinary family" plan for the evening. He remembered the last time Cherie had tried to cook.

Inside the supermarket, Cherie seemed quite lost, so Krystle steered her mother to the frozen meats. When they got there, a woman and her scruffy little boy were in the way, so Krystle shoved them out of it.

"Get a move on, Mum," she said. "Three steak mignon is all we want."

"Can't you find them for Mummy?" simpered Cherie. "Mummy might break her nails."

"Excuse *me*," said the woman who had been pushed aside, "but if you'll recall, we were here first."

"So whaddya want?" called Krystle, riffling through the cheap end of the freezer. "Portion of crummy mince? Crummy neck of crummy lamb?"

"Certainly not," answered Muriel Murray in a dignified fashion. "As a matter of fact, we're looking for steak mignon too."

Keith's mouth fell open. "No, we're not, Mum," he spluttered, wondering whether she had taken leave of her senses. "You said mince."

"For the dog, Keithie," said Muriel, digging him in the ribs.

"What dog?"

"Will you shut up?" hissed Muriel, pulling him aside. "This lady and her daughter are just the sort of classy people we need to get to know." And she smiled glassily at Cherie.

"They're not the sort of people *I'd* ever want to know," muttered Keith.

9

"Just shut up and smile," warned Muriel. She cleared her throat and said loudly to Cherie, "I don't think we've had the pleasure of meeting. We've just moved into the area."

"Reelly?" said Cherie without interest.

"Oh yeah?" said Krystle.

"Cherrytree Close," continued Muriel, in the plummy tone of voice she generally reserved for Keith's teachers at Parents' Evening. "Do you know it? 'Distinctive dwellings for the smaller family'."

Krystle and her mother exchanged a look. "Know it?" snorted Krystle. "My dad built it."

"Oh yeah?" said Keith. "Bricklayer, is he?"

Krystle turned quite white with rage. "He's a *multi-millionaire*," she squealed.

Meanwhile outside, Morris, tired of circling around, was trying to reverse the Maxi. The car park was still full, and there was little room for manoeuvre. But he thought he was doing reasonably well – until there was a loud *crunch*.

When Keith and his mother appeared from the supermarket, they found Morris being threatened by a big man in a leather overcoat. Apparently there had been some kind of accident between Morris's rusty heap and the big man's white Rolls-Royce. The hatchback of the Maxi had come open, and Golightly's Garden Gnomes had spilt all over the tarmac.

"Two thousand quid! That's how much it'll cost to put this lot straight," raged the big man, pointing to a tiny dent in the Rolls.

Morris, who didn't have two pounds to spare,

let alone two thousand, was more concerned with the state of his gnomes. Many had lost their fishing rods, some even their heads.

There might have been quite a nasty scene, had not the Crawley and Murray shoppers arrived just at that moment.

"What's your dad up to now?" grumbled Muriel to Keith. "Five minutes in what's supposed to be our new neighbourhood, and he's in trouble."

"My card," snorted J.C.B., pressing an embossed bit of pasteboard into Morris's hand, before he took the steaks from Krystle and chucked them into the back of the Rolls.

Muriel Murray peered over her husband's shoulder, and gasped: "Not *the* Crawley, of Crawleyhomes?"

"The very same," said J.C.B. grandly. "You'll be hearing from my people about the damage."

Keith was amazed to see his mother offer the millionaire her hand. "Madame Muriel du Maurier," she said gracefully.

"Madame *what*?" spluttered Keith.

An elbow nudged him to be quiet. "It was my professional name," hissed his mum. She turned to J.C.B. again. "Principal of the Du Maurier School of Dancing," she said poshly.

"D'you hear that, dahlin'?" said Cherie Crawley through her lip gloss.

"I hear it, doll," said J.C.B.

"Our little princess'd love to go there," said Cherie.

"Oh no I flamin' wouldn't," shouted Krystle.

"Oh yes you flamin' would," barked her dad. He turned to Morris Murray and offered him an unbelievably big cigar. "Forget about the dent, old

11

son. Your good lady here might just be the answer to our prayers."

"Right ho," said Morris, who was trying to fit the head back on a gnome.

"We've never really liked packing our princess off to them, er, those boarding schools, have we, Jay?" said Cherie, fluttering her sooty, stuck-on eyelashes.

"Nope," said J.C.B. "And what Madame – er – here seems to be offering— "

" —is a showbiz education on your doorstep, yeah?" said Cherie hopefully.

"You're not seriously enrolling me in her crummy rotten dancing school, are you?" fumed Krystle. "*Are* you? ARE you?"

3

Dance, Little Lady

"I AM NOT GOING TO WEAR *THOSE*!" screamed Keith, flinging the dancing shoes at his mother.

"Just this once, Keithie dear," pleaded Muriel. "By next Saturday I'll have found some more kiddies, but today I need you to be a little ballet-boy to her Sugar-plum Fairy."

The garage, which was the only room at Cherrytree Close big enough for the dancing class, had been cleared of the packing cases left by the removal men, and Morris had put up a hand-painted sign outside the house:

ACADEMY OF DANCE
Principal: Madame M. Du Maurier
Classical Ballet and Tap

Underneath, Morris had also written: "Golightly's Garden Gnomes on sale here", but Muriel had made him paint it out.

* * *

13

"You don't think *he'll* be there, do you, Dad?" said Krystle Crawley to J.C.B., as he drove her to 17 Cherrytree Close.

"Who's that, Princess?" asked J.C.B., lost in the maze of identical streets his company had built.

"You know, that horrible little boy," said Krystle. "No way am I gonna dance with *him*."

"You don't think they've forgotten, do you?" Muriel was fretting. Clad in lime-green leotard and tights, she was standing anxiously outside number seventeen, looking like an elongated frog. Morris, who was gluing a gnome back together, said nothing.

Muriel realised that the Crawleys were expecting a real stage school, not just dancing classes. But Keith wasn't starting school in Wibberley till September, and it was only July, so maybe she could have a go at running a stage school with him and Krystle as the first pupils. The sky was the limit – except for having Morris around the place when she was trying to make a good impression.

"You could at least have shifted that rust heap," she said, pointing at the car. "It lowers the tone, Morris." As if the tone weren't low enough already, she thought to herself, having to share her school of dancing with a load of garden gnomes.

Morris put down his glue, and searched for the car keys. Rather to his surprise, the engine started first time. With much grinding of gears (which caused the furry animals dangling from the windscreen to wobble wildly), he backed along the road, past the piles of builders' junk – and, with a *crunch*, went straight into the white Rolls which had just turned into Cherrytree Close.

14

"Sorry, squire," called out Morris. J.C.B. lowered his electric window and gave Morris a look that would have killed a more sensitive man.

"Hit him, Dad!" shouted Krystle from the passenger seat. She liked a fight.

"Why, if it isn't little Christine," called Muriel, rushing out to smooth the situation. "Come along, dear," she added, seizing Krystle. "Let's leave the silly men to sort everything out. Not brought any dancing shoes, I see?" Krystle wriggled under her grip, and said nothing. "Never mind, dear," went on Muriel. "You'll find plenty of second-hand ones in a big box upstairs."

Krystle had never worn anything second-hand in her life, and had no intention of starting now. But "upstairs" suggested the possibility of mischief, so up she went. At the top, she saw Keith peering round the door of his miniscule bedroom. She stuck her tongue out at him. Keith banged the door shut.

"Everything all right up there, my little loves?" called Muriel.

Krystle tried the door. Keith was holding on to the handle, but with one kick from Krystle it flew open.

"This the broom cupboard?" Krystle said, looking into the tiny room.

"Your dad built this rubbish," said Keith. "Anyway, I'm surprised at you showing up. Too much of a snob to come round here, I reckoned."

"Don't worry, little boy," said Krystle, sneering at the pinned-up portraits of Liverpool Football Club. "I've no intention of staying around." And she reached for the clasp on Keith's window. It opened wide. "Just as I thought," she said. "Same as all the others. Drain-pipe down to flat roof, then it's just a small drop to the ground."

Keith stared. "You're not going out by the window?"

"Aren't I just?" grinned Krystle.

"You wouldn't dare."

"Wouldn't I? I climbed down three windows from our dorm last term." She stuck a leg out on to the sill.

"You mean you're really ducking out?"

"Well, I'm not hanging about for all that ballet rubbish, least of all with the likes of you."

From downstairs wafted the sound of rather wobbly ballet music. Muriel had put on the record player. "Christine! Keith!" she called. But Krystle had already slung herself out on to the drainpipe, and begun to shin down.

"Where are you going?" gasped Keith, somewhat impressed.

"Far away from you lot as I can get. No 'beginners' ballet' for me."

"Me neither," said Keith suddenly, wondering where his new-found bravery had come from. "Wait for me!"

4

Down Town

To begin with, Krystle was furious with him for following. Thanks to the slippery soles of his dancing shoes, he had fallen rather than climbed off the one-storey flat roof, and was now limping.

"No one invited you along," she said crossly, as he hobbled painfully behind.

At first they were quite lost, scrambling over the building sites and empty houses that surrounded Cherrytree Close, but eventually they spotted the main road leading into the town. Krystle was still in half a mind as to whether to shake Keith off or not, but after a while she let him limp alongside her.

"Where are we going?" he asked.

"Dunno. Anywhere. Down the town. You got any money?"

Keith shook his head. "My pocket money was due. But with the move, Mum said I'd have to wait."

"How much d'you get?"

"Forty pee a week," said Keith. Krystle threw her head back and laughed. Keith reddened. "Why, how much do *you* get?" he asked.

17

"Pounds and pounds, as much as I want. Look, there's a bus." She began to run.

"But we haven't got any money," panted Keith, running as fast as his limp would allow.

The bus had stopped at some roadworks, where there were temporary traffic lights. The driver had opened the doors to let someone off, so Krystle and Keith sneaked on through the exit door.

"This is where they're building the new motorway," said Krystle. "When it's finished, you'll be able to get to London at about two hundred miles an hour. Not in *your* old car, though," she added.

The lights changed and the bus moved off. As they reached the next stop, the driver spotted them, and made them get off. When Krystle refused, he threatened to call the police, so they ran.

Krystle wanted to play the same trick all over again with another bus, and Keith wanted to go home, but in the end they decided to walk the rest of the way into town.

Twenty minutes later they were standing in the middle of the Wibberley shopping centre.

"Shopping mall, my dad calls it," said Krystle. She spoke it to rhyme with *hall*. "It's an American word, of course, but round here they're just too stupid to understand it."

"What's this place got to do with your dad?" said Keith.

"*He* built it, didn't he, Dumbo? And he owns it. Look." She pointed up to where a big sign announced that this was the CRAWLEY CENTRE.

Keith looked around him, at shops with names like Sox Box and Teen Seen, the same shops he'd seen where he used to live, the shops that advertised all the time on the telly, the same shops you could find all over the country. "You mean he owns all these?" he asked. "He must be stinking rich."

"He doesn't own the companies that run those shops, you dope. But he owns the building, and the companies pay him rent, and yes, he is stinking rich, and he gives me everything I want."

"Fat lot of good that is if you haven't any money now," observed Keith.

"I wouldn't buy anything here if I had," sneered Krystle. "It's just rubbish here. We get all our stuff in London."

"Show-off," said Keith. "Anyway, the stuff in London is just the same as this. It's the same everywhere."

"It'd be nice if we had the dosh to get something to eat," admitted Krystle.

There was a burger bar called the Merrie Muncher, and a pub in olde Englishe style called the Corne Dollie.

Then Keith's hand closed on something in his pocket. "Hey look, I've found fifty pence left over from school dinners," he said. "We *can* get something."

All they could get for fifty pence was a can of Diet Coke. They looked for somewhere to sit down and drink it, but there were no benches in the Crawley Centre.

An automatic door led to the outside world, where they found a bench overlooking a multi-storey car park. There were a few trees, but there were scarcely any leaves on them, even though it was July. Plastic bags had blown into the branches, and people had scrawled football slogans and rude graffiti all over the concrete walls. A wind blew between the tall concrete buildings. Krystle shivered as Keith opened the can of Diet Coke.

"I don't want your rotten germs," said Krystle. But she took the can off him, wiped the top, and had a few gulps. "The food looked crummy anyway," she said. "Like everything else in this crummy town."

"You're right enough there," said a shabby old man, sitting down at the other end of the bench. "Should've left it eighty years ago, instead of staying here all me life."

Krystle ignored the old man, but Keith, to be polite, said: "Has it always been like this?"

The old man shook his head. "Used to be a decent sort of place to look at, before they built this dump. But there's always been a bunch of stupid Herberts in charge of everything. That's how this rubbish got built."

Krystle shot him an icy glare. "C'mon!" she hissed. But Keith didn't move.

"Where we're sitting now," the old man was saying, "was the market. Just a lot of sheep, pigs and cattle, but it had character, you knows what I mean, atmosphere. More than you can say for this heap."

"We have to be going now," said Keith.

"And there was shops here too," continued the old man. "Not like this loada junk. Little shops with real people in them, who knew everyone, and served you with a smile. And the stuff they sold was stuff people needed. Not this American rubbish . . . "

"It sounds very nice," said Keith, getting up.

"And there was a proper railway station here, with trains with clean carriages. There was a theatre an' all, and a little hotel . . . "

"Really?" said Keith.

"And now they've pulled it all down," said the old man, "and put up this plastic and chrome American junk. Progress, they calls it. Ruination, I say."

"Yes, well, we really do have to be going now," said Keith.

"See you again," said the old man.

"Yes, er, ta-ta," said Keith.

5

Scenes from Shakespeare

As they walked, Krystle scrunched up the empty
Diet Coke can and began to kick it. Keith supposed
his mum must be panicking about them. He decided
to go home whether or not Krystle would come.

"I've heard about people like you," he said to
her. "You're bored because you've got too much
money."

"I'm bored because I have to hang about with
jerks like you."

They were walking past the multi-storey car park.
"My dad owns that," said Krystle.

Keith said nothing. Behind the car park was a big
new office building with "100,000 sq ft of fabulous
new office space to let" on it. "My dad built that,"
said Krystle.

They turned into a side street that led back into
the main road. "I bet your dad doesn't own *that*,"
Keith said suddenly.

"What?"

"That." He was pointing at a crumbling old building
on the corner of the street.

"I bet he does. He owns everything round here."

"Go on," said Keith. "What'd he want with an old eyesore like that?"

It certainly wasn't much of a sight at ground level, with torn posters flapping from its boarded-up front. But the top half of the building was completely different. It resembled a palace in a Walt Disney movie, with a gallery along the front, from which you might expect a king and queen to wave to the crowds. Above the gallery it was even grander, with bobbles and spikes, and fancy stonework with lettering that said "Theatre Royal".

"It's a theatre," said Keith. "The old man said there'd been a theatre."

"A dump like that," sneered Krystle, "and they call it the Theatre Royal!"

At the side of the building hung an old sign that said "Stage Door".

"Look," said Keith.

On the stage door were the remains of a faded poster:

For Five Nights Only
Commencing Monday 1 December 1890
The THEATRE ROYAL, Wibberley-on-the-Wold
(Proprietor & Gen. Manager: F. Scroggs)
Proudly Presents

The rest of the poster was missing.

"Eighteen-ninety," said Keith. "That's a hundred years ago."

"So it is, Dumbo."

"I reckon it might still be a real theatre inside."

"Look," said Krystle, "if I hear one more word

about that flaming theatre, I shall *puke*, right? And I ought to warn you, I'm really good at puking. At my last convent school, I was the champion puker. I used to throw up every lunchtime. In fact that's one of the reasons the nuns chucked me out," she added proudly.

Keith wasn't really listening. "The stage door doesn't look very secure to me," he said. "We could get in there, I reckon."

"You wouldn't dare," said Krystle.

"Who wouldn't?"

"You wouldn't!"

"Yes, I would."

"C'mon then."

The door was stronger than it looked. Keith tried the handle, but he couldn't make it budge. "Oh well," he said, trying not to sound relieved, "let's go then."

"Wimp," said Krystle.

"Well, *you* couldn't do it."

"Course I can." She put her shoulder to the door and shoved. Nothing happened. She shoved again and suddenly it burst open.

"Well, in you go, then," said Krystle. "Like you said you would."

"I'm going home," said Keith.

"Who's a little wimpy, then?" sneered Krystle. "And you just watch, 'cos *I'm* going in." She took a few small steps inside. "Cor," came her voice, "it really stinks in here."

"Okay, then, wait for me," said Keith. "I'm coming in too." He went through the door carefully, holding his nose.

It was very dark, and at first he couldn't see a

thing. When he got used to the darkness he managed to make out a staircase going up, and another going down.

"Not frightened of de dark, diddums, are we?" came Krystle's voice from somewhere in the blackness. Keith decided to ignore her, and simply look around.

He appeared to be in some sort of passage, which must be at the back of the stage. Gradually his eyes began to get used to the dark.

"Nothing here at all," he called out.

"Ickle baby wants diddums mumma."

"Oh, shut up."

He could see the stairs clearly now, and a door that probably led on to the stage. There was an old notice board, and on it was pinned the same poster they'd seen outside the stage door. This time the whole poster was there. After "Proudly Presents", it said:

WILLOUGHBY WELLINGTON
Great Britain's Leading Tragedian
and
Interpreter of the Bard
in
SCENES FROM SHAKESPEARE
Assisted by Bert Boot
BOOK EARLY TO AVOID DISAPPOINTMENT

In the middle of the poster was a drawing of an actor dressed in a crown and waving a sword. At the bottom, much smaller, was another drawing, of a little man in a battered top hat, grinning wildly.

Krystle brushed past him and went outside. "Cor," he heard her say, "what a stinking rotten place."

Keith followed her outside. "Found another poster," he said.

"What a clever little wimp."

"Oh, shut up, you. Bet you wouldn't dare go *right* in, beyond that passage."

"Yeah?" snapped Krystle. "And who says?"

"Okay then, go on."

"Don't worry," said Krystle, "I'm going." She went inside again. Keith followed.

He had forgotten to hold his nose this time, and suddenly the smell hit him – the smell of dust and damp and all the other smells a disused building gives off. "Ugh," said Keith, but he said it quietly.

Krystle was already trying the door that led from the passage to whatever was beyond. "It's no good without a torch," she said, pushing it open.

Keith felt inside the door. There wasn't a light switch. Everything inside was black and smelt even worse. "Let's go home," he said.

"Only a complete wally," said Krystle, "would get this far and give up." But she didn't seem to be in too much of a hurry to go through the door herself, into the blackness beyond.

"We don't know what's in there," said Keith. "There could be a dirty great hole, with a drop right down into the basement. You could fall down that and break your neck."

"There's a trick I know," said Krystle, "for seeing in the dark. I used it when I ran away from a school that was in the middle of the country. You just shut your eyes and count up to a hundred, and when you

26

open them again you'll be able to see more clearly. Let's try it. We've got to count right to a hundred or it won't work."

They stood by the door and shut their eyes and counted. "A hundred," said Krystle after a few moments.

"I've only got to sixty."

"Typical. Oh, come *on*." And she stepped boldly through the door.

"I can see all right now," came her voice. "It's no big deal anyway, just the stage, that's all, some boring scenery and stuff."

Keith followed her through the door. The trick had worked, and he could see the stage and the space beyond, where the audience would have sat. The floor felt firm.

At the back of the stage hung a big sheet of canvas with the paint peeled almost entirely off it, but Keith could just make out the shape of a castle. Some cut-out trees were stacked in a corner.

"Scenes from Shakespeare," he said.

"What's that?"

"Scenery from Shakespeare's plays."

"Boring old Shakespeare," said Krystle. Her voice echoed a bit.

"It'd be fantastic if they opened this place up again," said Keith.

"No it wouldn't. No one wants to see boring old Shakespeare except wimps like you."

"It wouldn't have to be Shakespeare, they could have pantomimes and things, and pop concerts."

"You must be joking, a pop concert in a dump like this?"

27

There was a noise behind them, something like a footstep. They jumped.

After a time, Keith whispered, "Did you hear something?"

Krystle shrugged. "Just the wind."

"There isn't any wind today."

"Then what else could it be? Was it *ghosties*, little Keithie?" she sneered.

"Shut up."

"Shut up yourself."

Crossly, Keith marched across the stage and out into the passage. The stage door had blown almost shut.

"Of course it was the wind," said Krystle, who had followed him. "Just a draught banging the door."

Keith went out into the daylight. It was good to smell the fresh air again.

He was surprised that Krystle hadn't followed him out. "Come on," he called.

After a moment, she appeared. She was looking rather white. "What's up with you?" sneered Keith. "Seen a ghost?"

"You just shut up," said Krystle, adding as an afterthought, "*wimp*."

6

Lost and Found

"What do *you* think, Morris?" said Muriel Murray in a panic-stricken voice, as her husband drove their rusting heap one more time around the maze of one-way streets that made up Wibberley's town centre. "*I* reckon they've been . . . kidnapped . . . that's what I reckon," she concluded tearfully.

"But who'd want to kidnap our Keith?" said Morris, as the car mounted the pavement and nudged a few bollards.

"It wouldn't be our little darling they were after," said Muriel, her blue-smudgy eye-shadow now covering her one lace hanky. "But *she'd* fetch a fortune in ransom money, she would . . . And I don't know what you're driving around for, Morris," she added disconsolately, " 'cos we're not going to find them just driving, are we?"

"Why's everybody hooting at me?" said Morris.

"Because you're in a bus lane, that's why."

"I'm always getting into bus lanes," said Morris. "How I hate this rotten, ruddy town."

"Well, it was your bright idea to move here," shouted Muriel, as Morris's car suddenly shot off down a pedestrian precinct.

Meanwhile Mrs Cherie Crawley was lying in a reclining chair, having her toenails revarnished in a manicurist's called Fingertips in the Crawley Centre. "Course, everyone's quite insistent that my Krystle's gonna make a lovely little dancer," she observed to Dawn, who was the girl looking after her.

"Oh yeah?" said Dawn.

"Yeah," said Cherie. "Course, she's got *my* legs." She lit a cigarette. "Her father and I have enrolled her at the academy of Madame du Maurier," she boasted.

"That in France, is it?" asked Dawn.

Cherie Crawley glanced up to see, in the mirror, the reflection of a rusty old car driving through the Crawley Centre. She blinked. She thought she had glimpsed Madame du Maurier's face in the car. And what was a car doing in here, anyway?

"Lot of people around here, aren't there?" observed Morris, as the car passed through the Crawley Centre. He looked in his cracked mirror and saw a swarm of uniformed security men running behind, shouting at him and waving their arms. "Can you see the way out of here, dear?" he asked Muriel, peering through the windscreen. The car appeared to be heading for an escalator.

Muriel put her hands over her face and screamed. At the last minute, just before the escalator, Morris swung the wheel to the right. The car dived through an automatic door, just missing two pushchairs, a nun, and a punk with green hair.

"I thought I spotted Mrs Crawley in one of those shops," said Morris, as the car bowled down a ramp, causing an abandoned supermarket trolley to career wildly in front of it, and making a terrified old lady scuttle for safety. "We could always stop and ask her if she's seen them," he suggested.

"Don't be ridiculous," shrieked Muriel. "It's her child we've lost." Then, "Look! It's *them!*"

Sure enough, Keith and Krystle were trailing along the pavement.

"Keithie! My baby!" squealed Muriel, hurling herself out of the car and rushing to clasp him to her.

Though they were embarrassed at Muriel's tearful welcome, the kids seemed quite glad to be picked up. Keith was limping in his ballet shoes, and Krystle seemed unusually quiet and pale.

By the time they got back to Cherrytree Close, everything was back to normal. Muriel had stopped calling Keith her little baby, and had resumed scolding Morris. Krystle was snapping at Keith just as usual.

Nevertheless, Keith thought there was something on her mind. Sure enough, when they were cleaning the dust and dirt of the theatre off themselves in the tiny bathroom, Krystle suddenly said, "You know, back there . . . just now . . . " She stopped.

"You know, back there, just *what?*" mocked Keith, throwing his ballet shoes in the frilly bathroom dustbin.

"Well," said Krystle, taking a deep breath.

"Well what?"

"I really did see a ghost," said Krystle.

Keith laughed so much that he fell against his mum's crinoline-lady-covered toilet roll.

After Krystle had been collected by her father's chauffeur, Muriel made tea, and insisted that Keith

31

tell her the whole story, which he did, except the bit about Krystle saying she'd seen a ghost.

"That child is a wilful little girl," Muriel concluded when she had heard it. "And dreadfully spoilt, too. But I'm surprised at you letting her lead you astray like that. You've always been Mummy's good little boy, haven't you?"

Keith made a face, but his mouth was too full of custard creams for him to reply. After a while he said, through another mouthful, "The theatre wath greath, though."

"Was it, sweetikins?" said Muriel, looking thoughtful. Keith described it to her in detail – the big stage with the scenery still standing there – and Muriel's blue-smudged eyes began to light up.

"D'you hear that, Morris?" she said, waving a custard cream at her husband. Morris, who felt he was somehow still being blamed for the children's disappearance, pretended not to hear, and went on trying to write an advertisement for his gnomes. "It could be just the thing, couldn't it?" went on Muriel. "A proper home for my dance academy. Keithie, we're going to see your theatre, right away!"

Half an hour later, Morris dropped Muriel and Keith on the corner by the Theatre Royal. "See you both in half an hour," he said.

"Where's Dad going?" asked Keith.

"To see a man about those perishing gnomes. Now, if I could get this theatre of yours up and running," dreamed Muriel, "he could forget all about them . . . Where is the theatre, Keithie?" she asked, spinning round on her stiletto heels and peering down the dingy, deserted street.

32

"You're standing in front of it, Mum."

Muriel looked up at the old building. "This . . . dump?" she gasped.

"It's not that bad when you get inside," said Keith. "C'mon."

The stage door was still open, just as they had left it. Muriel poked her nose inside. "I'm not going in there, Keithie. It's all pongy and filthy."

"Yeah, I know," said Keith, remembering how house-proud his mother was. "But it's great inside. It doesn't need that much doing to it," he added pleadingly.

"Well, at least we should have brought a torch," said Muriel, peering into the gloom. "That's another thing your father lost in the move."

"There's an electrical shop in the next street," said Keith eagerly. "You could always pop along and buy a cheap one."

When she had gone, Keith waited for a few moments. Then he went in through the stage door.

It did not seem so dark inside this time, but that was because he knew what was there. He went quickly along the passage and on to the stage. Then, more gingerly, he walked across the stage towards the front.

The stage came to an end abruptly, and he could not see what lay beyond it. He turned to go back to the door . . . and froze. Someone was standing on the stage.

It was a very tall man in a crown and a flowing robe, holding a sword. Keith stared, and the man stared back.

"Keithieeee!" It was his mother's familiar whiny

voice coming from the direction of the stage door. "You in there, Keithieeee?"

The figure and Keith stared at each other. Then suddenly the figure simply faded away. Where it had been standing, there was nothing.

Keith ran.

"What's the matter with you?" said Muriel, as he crashed through the stage door out into the daylight. "You look as if you've seen a ghost. The shop was shut, and really, Keithie, this place is too grubby for words. Let's hope your dad comes and picks us up quick, I want to go home."

A week passed, and 17 Cherrytree Close began to look a bit more homely, as Muriel organised the family's bits of familiar if worn-out furniture, and Keith pinned up more football pictures in his bedroom. Morris, who despite his expectations had not yet managed to sell any gnomes, kept as much out of sight as possible. Muriel managed to find two more pupils for the dancing class, which was to be held each Saturday morning – though she still lived in hopes of running a five-days-a-week stage school.

"Surely you don't need me for the dance class any more, Mum?" pleaded Keith. "Not now there's two more girls?"

But Muriel insisted.

"I can't even *dance*, Mum," he said. "Remember my limp."

"I didn't see any sign of a limp when you were kicking your football just now," snapped his mum.

"Oh, Mum . . . "

Keith hoped that Krystle wouldn't turn up again. He hated the sight of the bossy little horror. But sharp at ten on Saturday morning the white Rolls rolled into Cherrytree Close. Morris was dispatched to carry Krystle's posh little case, containing ballet shoes, ballet tights and hair net.

The class ended, in tears, at eleven.

The two new recruits, Zoe and Zara Thompson, were collected by an angry-looking mother, who whisked them off to bathe the shins which Krystle Crawley had kicked and the toes she had jumped on. Muriel, white-faced and near to tears herself, had gone up to her bedroom to recover, leaving Krystle and Keith to rip off their ballet things.

Morris brought a plate of Jaffa Cakes and some orange squash into the garage, where the gramophone was still playing a scratched recording of *Swan Lake*. "Hello, kiddies," he said. "Grub's up!"

Krystle took all the Jaffa Cakes. Keith wrestled with her and got one of them back for himself.

"You know that ghost business?" he asked when his father had gone again. "I've seen it too."

Krystle looked at him disbelievingly, but said nothing.

"Honest," Keith said. "I went back there with my mum."

"Baby Keithie had to take diddums mummy because diddums was frightened of ghostie."

"Oh, shut up," said Keith, turning his back on her. "Anyway," he added, "it was you that started this ghost thing."

Krystle said nothing, but stuffed in more Jaffa Cakes.

"I'm gonna go back there," went on Keith. "I'm gonna go back there this afternoon, Miss Posh

35

Vanity Case," he added, giving Krystle's case a little kick. "And of course Miss Posh Vanity Case is too *scared*."

"Who's scared, wimp? I'll be there at three o'clock."

7

Dummy

"Theatre?" said J.C.B. Crawley to his daughter, as the Rolls purred out of Cherrytree Close. "Watchoo want a theatre for, Princess, when you got the good old TV?"

They were driving back to Crawley Castle, the stately home just outside Wibberley which was J.C.B.'s business headquarters and home. It was a very ugly building, and J.C.B. had made it even uglier. He had knocked down the conservatory to make an indoor swimming pool, and had converted the chapel into a gambling casino for himself and his friends.

"I said, what's wrong with the TV?" he repeated.

"I'm bored with the telly," said Krystle.

"Get yourself some new videos, Princess."

"I'm bored with videos."

"Try some computer games."

"Boring old computer games."

J.C.B. sighed and lit another cigar. That was the trouble with young people today. They got bored so easily.

When they reached the motorway roadworks, the traffic lights were at red. While he waited, J.C.B.

dialled a number on his car-phone and started a business conversation about buying an old church and turning it into a three-in-one cinema. As he was talking, Krystle opened the door of the Rolls and slipped off, unnoticed by her father.

Keith found it harder to get away. He knew his mum wouldn't allow him out in the town again on his own – especially after his last escapade – so it needed an elaborate plan.

"The summer sales are on," he said brightly to Muriel. "I thought I might look for some new clothes for school."

"We haven't got the money," sighed Muriel, who was busily writing out advert cards for the dance school.

"I've got a bit in the Post Office," said Keith. "Dad could take me in."

Muriel sighed. She shouldn't let Keith spend anything when they were both so hard up, but she was glad that he was willing to use his money for school clothes, and if Morris drove him into town, it would be both of them out of her hair for a couple of hours. "Morris!" she shouted.

At the sound of his wife's imperious voice, Morris stopped dusting his gnomes in the garage and came to see what she wanted. He, too, was glad of an excuse to get out of the house.

"I won't be long, Dad," said Keith, as he leapt out of the car near the Crawley Centre. "See you here when you've parked." He was betting on his dad taking at least twenty minutes to park the car. Morris always got into a muddle in multi-storey car parks.

"All right, son. But I can't wait around all day,

mind. I've got a business to run." Dreaming of the day when he would be a really big name in garden gnomes – maybe a millionaire like that Crawley chap – Morris managed, at the fourth attempt, to get the Maxi into gear, and drove off.

It was already ten past three when Keith got to the theatre. Krystle was sitting on the step outside the stage door.

"You're late," she said.

"I haven't got long."

"Neither have I." She seemed less bad-tempered than usual, even a little nervous.

"Well, go on, what did you see?" asked Keith.

"I dunno. Just a face, I s'pose."

"A posh man in a crown, was it?"

Krystle shook her head.

"Well, where did you see it, then?" Keith asked. "On the stage?"

"In the passage. Peering down from the stairs."

"Mine was on the stage," whispered Keith, feeling wobbly in his stomach.

"Let's start searching around, then." But she didn't seem in any hurry.

"In the dark?" said Keith, hoping that they could call the whole thing off after all. "You gotta be joking."

"Guess who's nicked a couple of torches, then?" grinned Krystle. The torches had "Crawley Security Group" printed on them.

They pushed the stage door open and went in. The silence seemed to be listening to them. In the distance a police car went *nee-naw*, but otherwise it was unnaturally quiet.

"Where shall we start?" whispered Keith. "The stage?"

Krystle shrugged in agreement, and they went through the dark door into an open area.

"Nothing's been moved," whispered Keith, looking around him at the flaking scenery.

"Well why should it, thicko?" muttered Krystle.

With the torches it was possible to see beyond the stage, into the part where the audience had sat. The seats looked very dirty. There was an upstairs balcony with more seats.

"What about the stairs?" said Keith, a little louder than before. He was beginning to calm down a bit. "That's where you saw your ghost, wasn't it?"

"Dunno that it was a ghost really. Probably some mirror reflecting your ugly mug."

"Oh shut up," said Keith. "Do you want to look or don't you?"

"Might as well."

So they went into the passage and started up the stairs. These led up to a narrow passage like the one below. There was a row of doors with numbers on them. "Dressing rooms," said Keith.

"Know-all," muttered Krystle. She tried one of the doors, but it was locked. So were all the others.

"We could look in the basement," said Keith. "The stairs go down too, you know."

"They also go up another floor," said Krystle. Indeed, the narrow stairs vanished above them. So they went up.

Keith found himself leading. It was very dark on the stairs, and he was nervous of walking into giant cobwebs or something worse. At last they got to the top. The stairs ended at a small door. "Bet it's locked," he said, hoping it was.

But it wasn't. And the room into which it opened was quite extraordinary.

There were clothes everywhere, theatrical costumes, falling to pieces but still very beautiful and glamorous – kings' robes, queens' dresses, knights' armour, clowns' outfits, every imaginable kind of clothes. The whole place was covered in dust, but somehow it didn't feel quite as abandoned as the rest of the theatre.

It was quite light too. There was a big window, with a broad sill, on which were piles of stage "props" – artificial fruit, goblets and pewter plates, swords and crowns. The light streamed in, making the room seem altogether less sinister than the rest of the building.

"Wow, fantastic," breathed Keith, going over to look out of the window. "And wow, what a view. You can see right to the shopping centre, I mean, *mall*," he added, copying Krystle's American pronunciation.

"I don't know what you're getting so excited about," she sneered. "It's only a storeroom for boring old costumes."

"But just look at the tailors' dummies," said Keith.

There were six dummies in all, with costumes on each of them. One wore chain mail and a helmet, but had no face. The others all had faces, and were dressed as another soldier, a pantomime demon king, a yeoman of the guard, a witch, and a tramp in a battered hat.

Something about the last of them, the tramp, struck a chord in Keith's mind. He was wondering what it was when the tramp sneezed.

Keith and Krystle ran.

8

The Great Actor

It isn't easy being a ghost. It's thoroughly difficult to decide how to spend your day. Nevertheless, during all the years that Willoughby Wellington and Bert Boot had been ghosts-in-residence at the Theatre Royal, Wibberley-on-the-Wold, they had managed to organise the day into some sort of routine. At least, Willoughby Wellington, the "Great Actor", had managed to. He was the one who organised everything, the one who told Bert Boot what to do.

They would wake at six-thirty a.m. sharp. At least, Boot would wake then, because it isn't much fun lying in bed when you haven't got a bed to lie in. There *was* a bed in the wardrobe, the room at the top of the Theatre Royal where all the old costumes were kept, and where the ghosts had made their home. But Wellington always slept *in* it, and Boot *underneath* it.

"A great actor needs his sleep," Wellington would boom in his huge voice. "Otherwise how can he give of his best to his admiring audience, laddie?"

It was the voice with which Wellington had delivered his lines as Hamlet, Macbeth, wicked King Richard the Third, and all the other parts he had taken as the theatre's star actor years ago, before it closed down and he and Boot had starved to death.

Boot might have replied that, all those years ago, Wellington's audience hadn't always been admiring. Not by any means. How well he remembered the rotten cabbages and the tomatoes they would throw from the gallery on the nights when Wellington was particularly dreadful.

He might have. But he didn't. For Bert Boot was quite unable to speak.

This wasn't because he was a ghost. Wellington was a ghost too, and he could speak perfectly well. In fact all too well. He never stopped talking. But Boot had never spoken, not even when he was flesh and blood. He had spent a lifetime as an actor without being able to say a single line.

Probably he could have learnt to speak if his parents had talked to him when he was young. But they hadn't. His mother and father were circus clowns, and they had never said a word to each other, or to young Boot. They had just pulled funny faces, thrown buckets of water and flour over each other, and whacked each other with strings of sausages, and mimed things instead of saying them. So they hadn't taught young Boot how to speak.

He didn't care. As he grew up, he found it was easy to get people to understand him by making faces and miming like his parents.

When Boot had woken up, sharp at six-thirty, he would rub the sleep from his eyes, and go over to the window of the wardrobe to look out at the town. Every time he looked, Wibberley-on-the-Wold seemed to have sprouted some new building. He

43

longed to go out and see the place, because it had changed so much since he and Wellington had become ghosts. But Wellington always said "no" when Boot suggested it.

"A great actor does not go out to visit his audience," he would boom. "He must wait until his audience comes to see *him*. And come they will, laddie. They'll be here again soon, back in the stalls of the dear old Theatre Royal, cheering their hearts out as *I* come on stage. You just wait and see, laddie, you just wait and see."

Boot tried to point out (by miming) that the theatre had been closed and boarded up years ago, but Wellington paid no attention. So they never went outside, and Boot's only glimpses of the town, for years and years and years, had been through the wardrobe window.

As he stood at the window each morning, looking out rather sadly, and wishing he could go out and meet people, he would hear Wellington stirring in bed and calling for his breakfast.

He would sigh when this happened, because the breakfast thing was really very silly. Ghosts are quite unable to eat solid food. However, Wellington always insisted on having a pretend breakfast served to him in bed. "A great actor needs his food," he would boom. "One cannot give a great performance on an empty stomach, laddie."

Pulling a face to show how stupid he thought it was, Boot would put together a breakfast tray for Wellington. There was a bowl of wax fruit, a loaf of stage bread made of plaster of Paris, and an empty jug, together with a pewter plate that was really papier mâché, and a knife painted to look like gold, from the banquet scene in *Macbeth*.

When Boot had brought these, Wellington would spend about ten minutes in bed pretending to eat and drink, and calling loudly for "more hot coffee, laddie". Boot would pretend to bring it. Then Wellington would get out of bed and order Boot to dress him.

Some days he would choose to be dressed as Hamlet or Macbeth. That was all right for Boot, because the robes weren't too heavy (though they were falling to pieces with age), and he could manage them without too much difficulty. But if Wellington was in a bad mood, he would choose some horrid costume that took endless lacing up and adjusting, such as wicked King Richard the Third, (for which he wore a false hump and a wig of snake-like hair, not to mention a long nose made of putty, and rubber ears).

Worst of all, some days he decided to be dressed as Henry the Fifth, in full armour, including a visor which came down over his face. This took about an hour to put on, and Boot was always doing everything wrong, so that Wellington lost his temper and thrashed about inside, sometimes falling over because the armour was so heavy.

The next item in the ghosts' daily routine was fencing practice. This consisted of Wellington swinging a large sword wildly about the wardrobe, while shouting such Shakespearean lines as "Once more unto the breach, dear friends!", and "A horse! A horse! My kingdom for a horse!" Boot was meant to "parry", which meant fight back with his own sword. But the great actor hated being hit, even though, being a ghost, he couldn't feel a thing.

After fencing practice came elocution. This meant speaking. And of course all the speaking was done by Wellington.

Boot would have to go with him downstairs, to the dark and dusty theatre. Wellington would stand in the middle of the stage, and Boot would go to the back row of the stalls. His job was to listen while Wellington gave his voice its daily exercises. And this took hours and hours and hours.

"Arrround the rrrugged rrrocks the rrragged rrrascal rrran," pronounced the great actor in booming tones, rolling his r's, waiting for Boot to hold up his hand as a sign that he could hear every word. "Hooow nooow brooown cooow! Well, laddie, can you hear me?"

But by this time, Boot had usually fallen fast asleep out of boredom, and was snoring deeply.

After elocution, the great actor would retire to bed for his mid-morning snooze. During this, Boot was supposed to sweep the theatre, tidy up Wellington's clothes, and do all sorts of chores that the great actor had invented for him, though there didn't seem much point in them. After this he had to wake Wellington with "luncheon" – more pretend food.

Wellington would usually spend the afternoon making faces in a mirror. In his early days as a ghost, the great actor had tried to put on make-up, but make-up doesn't stick to ghosts, so he had to give this up as a bad job. In fact the afternoon was the worst time. Wellington often got very bored, and this made him very bad-tempered.

On the worst possible days, he would insist on changing his costume several times, so that Boot would spend hours and hours heaving clothes up and down the wardrobe, and trying not to lose things.

Also, as the years went by, the clothes fell more and more to pieces, so that it was getting very difficult for them to find anything Wellington could still wear. And this made the great actor even more bad-tempered.

At last, the evening came, and it was time for them both to go to bed – or at least for Wellington to go to bed, and for Boot to go under the bed. As he shut his eyes, he would sigh, and wish that something would happen to change this boring, tiring routine.

And now something *had* happened, and he was thoroughly frightened.

There had been noises in the theatre, and people, one of them a girl who said "Boring old Shakespeare!" Wellington, who had spent his life (and death) acting Shakespeare, had thought he was going to die of fury and misery when he heard this – except that he was dead already.

Boot, too, had been upset when he first heard the voices and saw the children. But then he'd been excited. It was wonderful to see someone new, someone different from the great actor who had been bossing him all these years. So he was very disappointed when Wellington, hearing the children come back, insisted that they hide upstairs in the wardrobe.

There was no need to hide, since they could both dematerialise – vanish – whenever they chose. But Wellington said he didn't want to see the children. And he made Boot come upstairs with him.

Wellington hid under the bed when he heard the children following them up the stairs, but Boot disguised himself as a tailor's dummy, so that he could have a good look at them. And now he had spoilt it all by sneezing. He supposed he would never see them again, but would be stuck with no company apart from the great actor for the rest of time. He felt absolutely miserable.

9

The Good Old Days

Keith and Krystle ran down the street from the theatre and round the corner to the shopping centre. They didn't pause till they reached the bench where Keith was supposed to meet his dad. There was no sign of Morris (who was still struggling in the multi-storey car park), but the old man who had spoken to them a week ago, when they had first explored the town, was sitting there, smoking his pipe.

Keith and Krystle were too out of breath to do anything except sit down and pant. "That's the stuff," said the old man. "Run round the town, breathe in the lovely traffic fumes!" Keith was too puffed to reply. "Come to think of it, you're both lookin' a bit grubby," went on the old man, who was none too spick-and-span himself. "And where in this town would you be able to pick up good old-fashioned dust like that on yer clothes, I wonder? Nowhere round here 'as been standin' long enough to be dusty, I'd 'ave thought."

"The . . . theatre," panted Keith.

The old man's eyes widened. "Ah," he said, "the *theatre*. The good ol' Theatre Royal. Now what, I

49

wonder, would you have been doin' around there?"

"None . . . of . . . your . . . business," panted Krystle rudely, but the old man paid no attention. Puffing at his pipe, he seemed to be talking to himself.

"Ah now," he said, "the Theatre Royal. Now that really *was* something. Finest theatre in this part of the country. And finest actors they thought theirselves. Leastways one of them did."

"Who was that?" asked Keith, getting his breath back.

The old man took another puff of his pipe. "Mr Willoughby Wellington," he said. "Famous Shakespearean actor."

"Boring old Shakespeare," muttered Krystle.

"Daresay you're right," said the old man. "But the way they used to do Shakespeare at the old Theatre Royal weren't ever boring. Oh dear me no, it was the funniest thing you've ever seen."

"Why was that?" asked Keith.

"Well you see," said the old codger, "it were the way things kept going wrong. Or rather, it were the way one little chap *made* them go wrong. I don't say it were on purpose, mind, but he did it so often you had to wonder."

"Who was that?" Keith asked.

"Funny little fellow called Bert Boot. I reckon he were only supposed to be the stage manager or odd job man or something, but maybe they was very short of actors (there weren't much money to go around), because he had to play a lot of parts. Indeed, as I recalls, usually there was just the two of them – Willoughby Wellington doin' all them great Shakespeare parts, like Hamlet and Macbeth and all

50

the kings, and this other little chap, Bert Boot, filling in the rest of the parts as best he could. And my, didn't he lead poor old Mr Wellington an awful dance!"

"Tell us about it," said Keith.

"Boring," muttered Krystle, but Keith could see that she was listening.

"Well," said the old man, "take that play about Hamlet. There's a bit in it when Prince Hamlet kills an old man what's hidin' behind a curtain, listenin' in to his conversation. Hamlet sees that curtain move, and makes a lunge at it with his sword, and stabs the old man. Well, whenever they got to that there scene, Wellington would say his line, something about spottin' a rat behind the curtain, and then he'd plunge in the sword. But while he were sayin' it, little Boot would move! Well of course he had to, not to get stuck with the sword. But he'd move a long way off, and stick his head round the curtain, and poke out his tongue at Mr Wellington! And Mr Wellington would get into a real rage then, and really lunge out with his sword. And they'd have a chase all over the place, and the audience would be screamin' with laughter. And finally Mr Wellington would decide to get on with the play, and he'd plunge his sword into the curtain for the last time, and then Boot would fall out from quite a different place, pretendin' to be dead! And that made everyone laugh till the tears ran down their faces! And Mr Wellington would come to the front of the stage, and shake his fist angrily, and that would make 'em laugh even more. Oh dear, oh dear, it were the funniest thing I ever saw!"

"Was that the only play that used to go wrong?" asked Keith.

"Lor bless you, no," said the old codger. "Nothin' ever went right when little Boot was around. The next play they did was *Macbeth*, and that was even worse – or better, dependin' on how you looked at it. The big bit in *Macbeth* is when old King Duncan is stabbed. The trouble were, Boot, who were playin' 'im, wouldn't lie down and die. He kept bouncin' up again, and wavin' at the audience and grinnin'. That spoilt poor old Mr Wellington's bits as Macbeth somethin' dreadful. But I think the best moment were in *Julius Caesar*."

"What happened there?" asked Keith.

"Well," said the old codger, "does you know the most famous line in that there play?"

"No," said Keith.

"Rotten old Shakespeare," said Krystle.

"It's 'Friends, Romans, countrymen, lend me your ears'," said the old man. "And when Mr Wellington speaks these words, on comes little Boot – in a pair of giant rubber ears, which he takes off and offers him!"

"I suppose it was things like that which made the theatre close down," said Keith. "I mean, the plays getting mucked up like that."

"Oh dear me no. The audience loved it, even if poor old Mr Willoughby Wellington didn't. No, the trouble started when Mr Wellington refused to act with Boot any more, and insisted on doin' shows all on his own. There wasn't much to laugh at then, so people mostly stayed away. Then, when movin' pictures was invented – what you'd call films – they tried runnin' the place as a picture house, a cinema. But there weren't anyone to work the projector except

Boot, and you can guess the sort of muddle he used to make of it. All the films shown upside down and back to front. So in the end the Scroggs family, they comes and shuts the place down."

"Scroggs?" said Krystle. "That's the name of the stupid old mayor."

"Aye," said the old codger. "The Scroggs's runs everything in Wibberley. Leastways they used to, before all this new rubbish came in."

"And who owns it nowadays?" asked Keith. "My mum wanted to use it for her dancing classes."

"Is that so?" said the old man, eyeing Keith rather oddly. "Oh, I wouldn't rightly like to say, though I reckon it can be discovered by any folks who takes the trouble."

"And how long ago did the theatre close?" asked Keith.

"Must be eighty-odd year ago," said the old man. "Maybe a bit more. I'm well past eighty myself, and I were only a toddler when I went to it."

"You saw them? Saw Wellington and Boot?"

"Oh aye. And I'll remember it till the day I dies. Never laughed so much since, I ain't."

"Would you know them if you saw them again?" asked Keith.

The old man smiled. "That I would. But such a thing ain't possible. They must 'ave died long ago."

"What happened to them after the theatre closed?"

"Nobody rightly knows. There were a story that they'd shut theirselves into the theatre. Some says they starved to death in there, and that their ghosts haunt the place to this day. Not that the likes of you would believe such nonsense." He got to his feet. "Well, I'd better be on me way."

"Goodbye," called Keith, as the old man ambled off.

Krystle said nothing.

Then, as an afterthought, Keith called out to the old man, "What's your name?"

"Scroggs," answered the old man.

10

Prestige Upgraded Executive Themed Retail Development

Meanwhile, Morris was having a bad time in the multi-storey car park.

He couldn't find a space for the Maxi; he couldn't understand all the instructions, and he started driving in the wrong direction.

People began to hoot and shout at him, and he became frightened, so he decided to get the car out again, back into the street. He managed to drive down to the ground floor again, though he went the wrong way, and people were still hooting. Then he saw what looked like the way out.

There was an automatic barrier with an arm that went up and down. The arm was just going up again, so he put the car into reverse and went backwards under the arm as fast as he could manage.

There was an enormous *crunch* as he hit something.

While Morris had been trying to park in the multi-storey, J.C.B. Crawley had discovered that Krystle was no longer sitting in the back of the Rolls. Cursing to himself, he turned the car round, and went back into Wibberley to look for her.

When he reached the multi-storey car park, he decided to park the car and search for her on foot. He was just driving past the automatic barrier when some lunatic drove backwards into him, with an enormous *crunch*.

J.C.B. Crawley was not usually at a loss for words, but when he discovered that the flaming idiot who had just reversed into him was the same flaming idiot who had bumped into his Rolls twice last week, it was a full fifteen seconds before the power of speech returned to him.

Morris, however, was perfectly able to talk. "Well, well, squire," he said cheerily to J.C.B., "fancy this happening again, eh? Still, coulda been worse, couldn't it, matey?"

J.C.B., his face contorted and purple, was still struggling for words.

"I mean to say," went on Morris, "one of us coulda had a nasty accident, eh?"

"A nasty accident's what's going to happen to *you* in a moment!" screamed J.C.B.

"Come, come, squire," said Morris sweetly. "It's my poor old Maxi what's got the dent." He patted the rusty end of his old heap, which, pitted as it was with the scars of other collisions, scarcely showed the mark of this latest bump. "Your posh white jobby's come off pretty well unscathed," went on Morris, tapping the bonnet of the Rolls. Its silver-plated radiator grille fell off with a clang. "I say, old man," he continued, peering at J.C.B. "You've gone a bit pale. Sure you're feeling all right?"

Morris would probably not have come out of the multi-storey alive if, at that moment, a bleeping sound

56

had not emerged from J.C.B.'s pocket. The millionaire whipped out his portable phone and answered it. The call was from his chief accountant, a man named Mr Herring. It was to summon him at once to Crawley Castle, where the men from the bank which lent Crawleyhomes money had called an emergency meeting.

J.C.B. put the phone back into his pocket and snarled at Morris, "You'll be hearing from my lawyers on Monday morning. I'll have you kept off the roads for the rest of your life." Then he got back into the Rolls and sped off.

The accident had caused more damage to the Rolls than he realised. The radiator was leaking water, and by the time the car reached the edge of the town, near the motorway works, it had run dry. Warning lights flashed as the car came to a halt.

Swearing to himself, J.C.B. dialled his office on the car-phone. But the car's electrical system seemed to have been affected by the radiator trouble, and the car-phone wouldn't work.

J.C.B. took out his pocket phone and tried again. This time he got through to the office. But all he heard was an answering machine telling him the office was closed, and would he please call back again on Monday morning.

He couldn't remember the number of Herring's direct phone-line, so he tried his own home number at the castle. This time he got another answering machine, on which Krystle had recorded a rude message: "This is stupid Crawley Castle and all my stupid family are out. No one wants to talk to you anyway."

In a rage, J.C.B. hurled the portable phone into the back of the Rolls. Then he realised he would have to phone for a taxi. But when he retrieved it, the portable phone wouldn't work any more.

Furiously, he climbed out of the Rolls, slammed the door, and began to walk the rest of the way home.

Crawley Castle wasn't a real castle, just a big ugly house pretending to be one. It had been built not very long ago by Ebenezer Scroggs, who had made lots of money brewing beer in Wibberley-on-the-Wold, and wanted to live in an Olde Englishe house. It looked about as much like a real castle as the Corne Dollie pub in the Crawley Centre looked like a real old pub, which is to say not at all.

J.C.B. had bought it from the Scroggs family when he started to make his fortune out of Crawleyhomes. At first he had intended to turn it into a country club and leisure centre, with a sauna, a miniature golf course, a gambling casino, and various bars and restaurants. But soon he was so rich that he could afford to live there himself.

He had a dream of what life would be like when all his plans for Wibberley-on-the-Wold were finished. There would be no old buildings left at all in the town, just brand-new houses and shops and offices, all built by his company. The entire countryside surrounding Wibberley would be filled with Crawleyhomes in all their varieties: big ones pretending to be olde worlde country cottages; little ones like tiny office blocks; crazy blocks of flats like mad Chinese pagodas.

There would be no more messy open fields and

woods, just every shape and size and type of brand-new Crawleyhome, each with its garage and patio and satellite TV dish. Gone would be the rolling fields and woodlands. For mile after mile would stretch the Crawleyhomes. And in the middle, towering above them all, would stand the mighty Crawley Castle, with himself as its king.

He reminded himself of this wonderful dream as he trudged wearily back to the castle – trudged through the mud and sludge of the motorway works, and past the sprawling untidy building sites where half-finished Crawleyhomes were still being erected. Lorries and cars zoomed by him, splashing him with mud. He tried thumbing a lift, but no one stopped. It began to rain.

About half an hour before this, Keith was still hanging around waiting for Morris to reappear from the multi-storey. "Can't think what's keeping Dad," he said to Krystle. "Shoulda been here ages ago."

"We could always go back to the theatre," said Krystle.

Keith stared at her. "Thought you said the theatre was boring."

"Shakespeare is boring. *Ghosts* aren't. Come on."

So back they went.

At Crawley Castle, a group of unsmiling bankers arrived precisely on time. Mr Herring was there to welcome them. Nervously, he explained that J.C.B. had been "detained at a previous meeting", and would be arriving shortly. He offered them champagne and cigars, which they refused. They unpacked their briefcases and sat at the board room table, drumming their fingers. They looked as if they were in a nasty mood.

After three quarters of an hour, the door opened, and in walked J.C.B. His shoes were covered with mud, his trousers were dirty, his shirt was dripping with rain, and his hair was plastered over his forehead in streaks.

"Hello, me ol' muckers," he said to the stony-faced bankers. "Bitta trouble on the road, doncha know. Herring, give me a pint of champagne. Now, what can I do for you fellas?"

The bankers said that Crawleyhomes owed them thirty million pounds. They wanted it back, and they wanted it quickly.

J.C.B. downed his pint of champagne and called for another. He lit a cigar.

"Listen, fellas," he said, "be reasonable. That thirty million was lent us so we could build a whole lotta new houses. Well, we're building them."

The bankers reminded him that the money had been lent for a year. The year was up, so they wanted the money back. If he had managed to sell the houses, he shouldn't have any trouble repaying the money.

J.C.B. finished his second pint of champagne. He didn't tell the bankers this, but the trouble was that nobody was buying Crawleyhomes any longer. The only house they had sold recently was one of those pitiful little things in Cherrytree Close – which had been bought by the bloke who kept smashing into him in the Maxi. Dozens and dozens of other new houses were standing empty, with "For Sale" signs in front of them.

So he couldn't repay the thirty million pounds.

He didn't tell the bankers that he couldn't give them back their thirty million. He just said, "I'll be in touch Monday morning, fellas. Don't worry, you'll get your thirty million right away. And it's been great meeting you."

He saw them out to their car.

When he got back, he said to Mr Herring, "Get me another thirty million by Monday morning."

Mr Herring turned pale. "How am I to do that, Mr Crawley?"

"I dunno," said J.C.B. "You're the flamin' accountant. You're s'posed to know about money, so flamin' get me some."

"I suppose we could always borrow it to finance some more buildings, Mr Crawley," said Mr Herring, feeling several dozen more grey hairs growing on his head. "We should be able to find some fool – I mean, some imaginative investor – who'll dish up thirty million if they think you need it for some exciting new project. Like, say, a new shopping centre for the town."

"Bonzo idea, Herring," said J.C.B. "A new shopping whatsit it is."

"What are you going to call it, Mr Crawley? The new project needs an exciting name if people are going to lend us money for it."

J.C.B. thought for a moment. "We could call it the New Shopping Centre," he said.

Mr Herring shook his head. "That won't do, Mr Crawley. 'New' isn't a trendy word any longer. The trendy words are things like 'prestige' and 'upgraded' and 'executive' and 'themed' and all that sort of thing. And people don't talk about shopping centres any longer, they talk about 'retail developments'."

"Okay," said J.C.B. "Sounds a loada rubbish to

me, but we'll call it the Prestige Upgraded Executive Themed Retail Development."

"If it's going to be 'themed', Mr Crawley, there has to be a theme."

"A theme?" said J.C.B. "What's a flamin' theme?"

"Surely you've heard of theme parks, Mr Crawley?" said Herring. "The idea began with Disneyland, and now they're all doing it. You have a Robin Hood theme, or a Star Wars theme, or something like that. All the stately homes do it. Come to think of it, there hasn't been a themed shopping centre – I mean, retail development. We could be breaking new ground."

"Okay," said J.C.B. "If it's going to raise us thirty million by Monday morning, we're going to be themed."

"But what sort of theme do you want, Mr Crawley? And where is it going to be built? We've already messed up – I mean, developed – most of the town already. Look." And Mr Herring fetched a map of Wibberley. Sure enough, almost all the town was coloured red, which meant that Crawleyhomes had built it.

"Wait a minute," said J.C.B. "There's a whole flamin' street behind the Crawley Centre we haven't touched."

"We never bothered with it," said Herring, "because it's so dingy down there. Just some tumbledown old houses and the remains of a theatre."

"Theatre?" said J.C.B. "My princess, my little Krystle, was talking to me about a theatre today. 'Daddy,' she said, 'I'm so bored with the telly, I want to go to the theatre.' Do you hear that, Herring? That's what the young people of today are saying.

62

And a theatre's what we're going to give them."

"Yes, Mr Crawley."

"And it won't be just any ordinary flamin' theatre, Herring. We're going to take that old theatre in Wibberley, Herring, and we're going to turn it into something special. We're going to turn it into a prestige upgraded executive themed retail development. A shopping centre themed as a theatre. And we're going to raise a loan of thirty million to finance it. Herring, get down to work. You've got to find who owns that flamin' theatre, and buy it at once."

11

How to Frighten a Ghost

"It's no good," said Keith. "We'll have to give up. We must have imagined the whole thing."

They had gone back to the theatre, hearts in mouths, and had tiptoed around, searching for the ghosts. But there was nothing to be seen anywhere. The room at the top of the stairs, where Keith thought he had seen Boot sneeze, showed no signs of occupation. The dusty costumes hung silently on their rails.

"I reckon there's been no one here since the place closed," Keith said gloomily. "Bet it was a rat or something I heard sneezing."

" 'spect it was," said Krystle.

But when they got back to the stage door, someone had written on the inside of it, with a stick of flesh-coloured make-up, a single word: "HELLO."

"Maybe it was there already," whispered Keith, "and we just didn't see it."

Krystle shrugged. "Looks mighty fresh to me."

"Okay," said Keith. "Let's give searching the place another try. *Hello*!" he called out loudly.

But there was no answer.

"We haven't tried the basement," whispered Krystle, pointing at the stairs.

"I'm not going down there," muttered Keith. "It's all dark and filthy."

"Little Baby Keithie," teased Krystle. But even she was nervous as she started down the stairs.

At the bottom it was almost pitch dark, but she could just make out a mirror hanging from a beam. Probably the actors had used it when changing costumes in a hurry.

She looked at herself in the mirror, but it was so dark that she couldn't see the reflection properly. There was something odd about it, but she couldn't say exactly what.

She raised her right arm. The figure in the mirror raised its arm too.

She waved. The figure in the mirror waved back.

She stuck out her tongue. The figure in the mirror thumbed its nose at her instead.

"Gotcha," she shouted, making a lunge at the mirror – which wasn't a mirror at all, but just an empty picture frame. But the person in the mirror vanished.

"Oh, no!" wailed Krystle. "I've only gone and frightened him!" She ran back upstairs. "I saw the funny one, Boot," she told Keith breathlessly, "but I frightened him and he, well, he just . . . vanished."

"Oh, terrific. You frightened him," said Keith furiously.

"It wasn't *my* fault . . . " She got her breath back. "If only we could make them realise we don't mean them any harm."

Keith suddenly took a sharp breath. "Look!" he said.

Down the stairs from the wardrobe, a piece of paper was floating in mid-air. When it reached the bottom of the stairs it stopped. Somebody invisible must be holding it.

His own hand trembling, Keith took the piece of paper and unfolded it. On it was written, in neat spidery writing:

> *Mr Willoughby Wellington,*
> *the celebrated Shakespearean tragedian,*
> *requests the pleasure of your company*
> *in the wardrobe, Theatre Royal,*
> *Wibberley-on-the-Wold*
> *at your earliest convenience.*
> *Refreshments will be served.*

"Hey! Look at this!" said Keith. "They want to meet us!"

"Race you," shouted Krystle, pushing past him up the stairs.

12

Theatre for Sale

Mr Tom Scroggs, the old man who had talked to Keith and Krystle on the bench outside the shopping centre, was looking through his collection of theatre programmes from years ago.

They were kept in a big scrapbook, with "Theatre Royal, Wibberley-on-the-Wold" printed on the front in gold lettering. Mr Scroggs looked after it carefully, because nowadays he was the owner of the Theatre Royal. It had been left to him by his uncle, Fred Scroggs, who had owned and managed it in the days when Wellington and Boot were performing there.

Mr Scroggs hadn't told Keith and Krystle that he owned the theatre, because he didn't tell anyone. He thought it was best to keep quiet about it. He was afraid that the people who had put up all the ugly new buildings in Wibberley would soon try to get their hands on it.

Sure enough, at that very moment Mr Herring was in the public library, looking up old documents to discover who owned the Theatre Royal. And half an hour later he was knocking on Mr Scroggs's front door.

Mr Scroggs peeped out and saw a weedy-looking fellow carrying a shiny plastic-and-metal briefcase. "There's no one in," he yelled.

Mr Herring tapped on the door again. "What d'you want?" shouted Mr Scroggs.

"Are you Thomas William Scroggs," called Mr Herring though the letterbox, "the owner of the Theatre Royal, Wibberley-on-the-Wold?"

"That's none of your business," shouted Mr Scroggs. "Buzz off!"

"I represent Crawleyhomes," called Mr Herring. "We would like to make you an offer of ten thousand pounds for your theatre."

"I've got a savage guard dog in 'ere," called Mr Scroggs, making barking noises.

"Twenty thousand then, Mr Scroggs."

"Woof woof."

"Fifty thousand."

"Woof. Grrrr."

"A hundred thousand."

Mr Scroggs went and filled a bucket with water and took it to the upstairs window.

"A hundred and fifty thousand, Mr Scroggs," called Mr Herring. "And we'll give you a free retirement apartment in Crawleyhaven, so you can 'grow old on the Wold'."

Mr Scroggs emptied the bucket of water over him.

Morris Murray had by now finally left the multi-storey car park and gone to look for Keith. He was not on the bench where they had arranged to meet, but an old woman said she had seen him and a girl talking to a Mr Tom Scroggs, who lived nearby.

When Morris drove up to Mr Scroggs's front door,

there was a puddle of water on the pavement, but no sign of Mr Herring, who had gone to fetch help.

Morris knocked on Mr Scroggs's door. "I won't sell, not for a million," yelled a voice.

"Is that Mr Scroggs?" called Morris. "Have you seen my lad, who you were talking to before?"

Mr Scroggs opened the front door. "How do," he said. "I thought you was an awful little feller with a plastic suitcase. Yes, I seen your lad, and the girl with 'im. Try the theatre, that's my guess where you'll find 'em."

"Thanks, old man," said Morris. Then a thought struck him. "I don't suppose you'd like to buy any gnomes, Mr Scroggs?"

"Gnomes?" said Mr Scroggs suspiciously.

"Golightly's Garden Gnomes. They come in all shapes and sizes. Cute little fellows, with fishing rods and toadstools and all that. I've got a box-full in the Maxi."

A smart car turned into the street, a white Rolls with the number-plate JCB 2 – the spare car from Crawley Castle.

Mr Scroggs saw it coming. "Tell you what, mister," he said to Morris, "there's somethin' I want to get off me hands in a hurry, before this lot forces it out of me. How'd you like to buy a theatre?"

By the time J.C.B. had parked the Rolls, and he and Herring (still dripping wet) had got out, Morris had driven off. "It's that lunatic in the Maxi again," fumed J.C.B. "Now, let's see what the power of cash can do."

J.C.B. had brought pocketfuls of banknotes with him, in the hope that the sight of real money would make this old Scroggs idiot change his mind.

Mr Scroggs was waiting on the front door step. "You're wastin' your time!" he shouted at J.C.B. "I've already sold the dratted theatre."

"Sold it?" gasped J.C.B. "Who to?"

"None of your business."

"What was the price?" said Mr Herring faintly. "How much did you sell it for?"

"I sold it," said Mr Scroggs triumphantly, "for a box of garden gnomes."

13

Tiny Tim

Boot had been having a terrible afternoon. As soon as he sneezed and the children had run away, Wellington had been furious with him for frightening them.

"They will go and fetch the police," he announced gloomily, "and then we shall be thrown into England's deepest dungeon."

Boot thought this was all nonsense, but he was upset that the boy and girl had run away. Also, Wellington had now decided that he liked the children – or what he had seen of them from beneath the bed, where he had been hiding. He told Boot that if they came back again without the police, he would make them welcome.

"They are the rising generation, laddie," he told Boot. "We must give them a taste of the excitement the theatre can offer."

Boot wondered what this meant, but he soon discovered. Wellington had decided that he was going to receive Keith and Krystle in costume. "Don't you understand, laddie?" he cried. "We are going to give them a performance!"

So Boot had spent half an hour struggling with a

mountain of costumes, as Wellington kept changing his mind about which part he would play.

"Wicked King Richard would terrify the poor babes," he mused. "Henry the Fifth is a noble part, but the visor of the helmet does get stuck over one's face, and 'twould be difficult to eat and drink." (He intended to serve a stage feast for the children.) "Julius Caesar would do fine, laddie, but the leaves on my laurel crown have all fallen off. Hamlet – maybe it should be Hamlet?"

He was still trying to make up his mind when there were noises downstairs. Boot peeped out. The children had returned.

"Keep them occupied," hissed Wellington. So for the next ten minutes, while Wellington climbed into his chosen costume, Boot did his best to stop the children from leaving again – writing HELLO on the stage door, and pretending to be a reflection in a mirror. At last everything was ready, and Boot invisibly carried to the children the invitation the great actor had written out. Then he scuttled back upstairs to be ready for them.

When the children knocked on the wardrobe door, it opened as if by magic (Boot was standing behind it), and mysterious music began to play (Boot had put a record on the theatre's old gramophone). There was nobody to be seen, but in the middle of the room a table had been laid with a sumptuous feast.

"*You know your own degrees, sit down*," boomed a voice from behind a curtain, "*At first and last the hearty welcome*." Krystle and Keith jumped at the sound (it was Wellington speaking lines from the banquet scene in *Macbeth*), but they sat down at the table.

"Thanks a lot," said Keith politely.

Krystle, who was examining the bowl of wax fruit and the loaf of plaster of Paris bread, said, "This isn't real food."

Behind his curtain, Wellington felt that things didn't seem to be going quite right. He waved frantically to Boot to put on the next record.

There was the sound of trumpets, and Wellington stepped out to reveal himself. He was wearing a tunic and tights sewn with silver sequins, but a lot of the sequins had fallen off, and there was a hole in one knee.

This was Prince Charming's costume from *Cinderella*, the last pantomime to be performed at the Theatre Royal before it closed. Wellington had decided he would recite the Prince's big speech. Stepping forward, he began:

> And now our story's soon to end,
> But where's the Prince's little friend,
> The beauteous girl who danced so well,
> But ran off at the chiming bell?
> I'll seek her up and down the land,
> And when I've found her, beg her hand.

He waited, as if expecting applause.

"Reckon that one's off his rocker," said Krystle.

"Ssh," said Keith, not wishing to cause offence.

Wellington was indeed most offended at the interruption, but he carried on regardless, booming his lines:

I've found her slipper made of glass;
The girl who wore it fled, alas,
And I must rack my mortal wits
To find her foot – the foot that fits!
First I must try the sisters twain;
From my grand ball they're home again.
Let's hope the slipper fits *them* not,
Else I an ugly wife have got!

He paused, looking expectantly around the room. "The *slipper!*" he hissed angrily.

From behind the curtain, a hand (it was Boot's, of course) passed him not a dainty glass slipper, but an enormous army boot. Wellington hurled it back in rage, while Krystle and Keith rocked with laughter.

Wellington cleared his throat angrily, and went on:

No, no, all's well, it is not theirs.
But who's this coming down the stairs?
'Tis far more beauteous than a fella –
The girl herself! It's Cinderella!

The curtain twitched aside, and in rushed Boot in a dress and a long yellow wig. He waved cheerily at the children and blew kisses at Wellington.

"Get off!" roared Wellington, while the children collapsed laughing.

"Bravo!" called Keith. "Encore!"

"Great!" shouted Krystle. "More!"

Boot began to bow wildly, taking off his wig and waving it about in the air. Wellington kicked him out of the way and glared at the children.

"Ladies and gentlemen," he said in a ringing voice,

"since you have done us the honour of calling for more, we now present something *very serious*, at which *nobody could possibly laugh*. This celebrated dramatic monologue has been performed before many crowned heads – or at least many mayors of Wibberley-on-the-Wold. I speak, of course, of that tragic tale of olden times, *The Crossing-Sweeper's Christmas*." And he motioned to Boot to put another record on the gramophone.

This time it was slow, sad music. After a few bars, Wellington began to recite in a sonorous voice, waving his hands about a lot as he spoke:

> 'Twas Christmas Day at the crossing,
> One Christmas in the past.
> The wind was rough and icy,
> And the snow was falling fast.

At this, Boot rushed up with a bucket and emptied paper "snow" all over Wellington. Keith and Krystle burst out laughing, but were silenced by a grim stare from the great actor. He went on with the next verse:

> Pity the crossing sweeper,
> A lad so frail and slim.
> Scarce thirteen summers was his age,
> And his name was Tiny Tim.
>
> Pity his poor old mother,
> A widow pale and worn,
> For to her boy she says goodbye
> At half-past five each morn.

At this moment, Boot appeared with a blanket over his head, imitating (with a toothy grin) a poor old woman waving goodbye. Krystle and Keith giggled, but managed not to laugh out loud. On went Wellington:

> The tiny lad was hungry,
> His mother's plight was grave.
> Nought in her purse, her larder bare,
> But what she had she gave.

From beneath his blanket, Boot produced an enormous string of rubber sausages and offered them to Wellington, who flung them back angrily at him, and did his best to carry on.

> Poor Tiny Tim, he worked all day
> A-sweeping of the street;
> He worked in rain, he worked in hail,
> He worked in driving sleet.

> That Christmas Day, the wind was cold;
> It blew both hard and strong.
> It blew from north, it blew from south,
> It blew the whole day long.

In a corner of the wardrobe, Boot began to turn the handle of a machine which imitated the sound of the wind. He turned it so hard that the noise became deafening, and Wellington had to shout the next verses:

> The ladies in their carriages,
> The yeoman on his steed,

They ride their way past Tiny Tim,
And no one pays him heed.

The sun goes down, the day is done,
The weather grows more cold,
And Tim would from a rich man beg,
If he dared be so bold.

At this, Boot marched on in a top hat, as a rich
man, while Wellington went on:

The rich man has a hardened heart,
Like others of his ilk,
He gives but little of his coin,
And little of his silk.

On the last line, Boot dived into his pocket and
offered Wellington a silk handkerchief. Wellington
took it, but it would not come away from Boot's
pocket. He tugged and tugged – whereupon yards
and yards of handkerchief began to emerge, like an
enormous rope. After he had pulled out about six feet
of it, Wellington gave up, and, kicking Boot out of the
way once more, continued with the poem – while Keith
and Krystle tried to stifle their laughter.

The sun goes down, the day is done,
The night it falls so chill.
And now, alas, the lad's strength wanes;
Poor boy, he's feeling ill.

Wellington sank to his feet, and his voice became
weak and feeble:

"Ah, Doctor! Doctor!" cried the lad,
"My last hour has begun.
"Ah, Doctor! Doctor! Save me now."
But doctor came there none.

Either Boot wasn't listening properly, or he had other ideas, for at this line he rushed on with a stethoscope round his neck and tried to force an enormous pill into Wellington's mouth. Furiously, Wellington pushed Boot out of the way. Grinning all over his face, Boot ran off.

The night has come,

Wellington recited,

the snow falls thick,

at which he turned just in time to prevent Boot tipping another bucket of "snow" over him,

The wind is worse than ever.
Poor Tim, he sinks upon the ground,
And rise again he'll never.

The night has come, Tim's heartbeat fades,
The clock it strikes eleven.

He waited expectantly, but nothing happened.

The *clock* it *strikes eleven*!

he repeated angrily. Finally, Boot picked up a large
handbell and rung it wildly. With his hands over his
ears to shut out the din, Wellington yelled the final
two lines of the poem:

> And as Tim dies, an angel comes
> And takes him up – to heaven!

With tears streaming down his cheeks, he stood
up and bowed, to the applause of Krystle and Keith.
But Boot hadn't finished. On he rushed in a long
nightgown, with wings tied to his back. The angel
had come to carry off Tiny Tim!

Wellington saw him coming, and tried to dodge
out of the way, but Boot wouldn't be stopped. Bowing
wildly to the children's applause, he kept making a
grab for Wellington. Finally he got hold of him, and
the two of them collapsed in a heap, bringing down
several rows of costumes with them. Krystle and Keith
had never laughed so much in their lives.

14

Morris Makes A Fortune

"Herring," said J.C.B., "somewhere in this town there's a bloke who's just swapped a box of garden gnomes for a theatre. And we gotta find him."

"Where are we going to start, Mr Crawley?" whined Herring, who was still damp from the bucket of water Mr Scroggs had thrown over him.

"There can't be many blokes going around with boxes of garden gnomes," said J.C.B. thoughtfully. "Come to think of it, I've run into one meself. Or rather, he's run into me. Three times. You won't believe this, Herring, but it's the bloke who keeps smashing into my Roller. The lunatic with the battered Maxi. It's full of gnomes. And *he* should be easier to find than a needle in a haystack. Come on." They got into the white Rolls, and sped off down the street.

No sooner had Morris set off from Mr Scroggs's house, with an old envelope on the front seat of the Maxi labelled "Deeds of ownership of Theatre Royal, Wibberley-on-the-Wold", than he realised he hadn't the faintest idea where the theatre was. He decided to go back and ask Mr Scroggs.

As it was a one-way street, he knew better than to turn the Maxi around. He simply backed it, rather fast, down the street.

The Maxi met the white Rolls, as it was coming *up* the street, with the usual *crunch*.

"I don't flamin' believe it!" yelled J.C.B. "Now he's ruined me *second* car. Still, at least we've found the blighter."

Meanwhile, back at 17 Cherrytree Close, Muriel Murray was wondering what had happened to the rest of the family. It seemed like hours since Morris had driven Keith into Wibberley to do some shopping. She looked at her watch. It *was* hours.

Wasn't that just like the men of the family, wandering off and leaving her to do all the work – writing advert cards for the dance school. The way Morris's gnomes business was going, the dance school would have to support them all.

She shut her eyes and began to dream. To dream of the Muriel du Maurier School of Dancing, her very own cute little dancers, starring in a production in some famous London theatre. Mind you, she thought, I needn't aim for London to start with. That old theatre in Wibberley may have possibilities after all. A dustpan and brush, and a good scrub, and the place mightn't look half bad. She could just imagine the front all done up to look smart, with her own name in lights . . .

The MURIEL DU MAURIER School of
Dancing in *Swan Lake* . . .
MADAME MURIEL DU MAURIER leads her
talented dance troupe in *Cats* . . .

The MURIEL DU MAURIER All-stars in *Grease*.

The front door of 17 Cherrytree Close opened, waking Muriel from her dream. It was Morris. But an odd-looking Morris. He seemed in high spirits.

"Wonderful news, dear!" he said brightly.

"Sold a gnome, have we?" said Muriel, yawning.

"Not just one gnome, dear, a whole boxful. And guess what I got for them?"

"Money, I hope," said Muriel languidly.

"No," said Morris. "A bundle of papers."

Muriel looked for a vase she didn't like, to throw at him. Honestly, Morris could be unfathomable at times.

"Not just any papers, my sweetness," said Morris, seeing the hand menacingly take aim. "Deeds of ownership, they were. Of the Theatre Royal, my petal."

If Muriel had been an excitable woman, she would have leapt up from their second-hand settee and hugged Morris.

"But then again," went on Morris, "I said to myself, Morris, old son, who wants a tumbledown theatre?"

Muriel reached for the vase again.

"And wasn't it just my good fortune," Morris continued, "that who should happen to come along but old Mister Midas himself, what's his name, old Creepy Crawley. And he gave me a hundred quid for 'em, didn't he, dear?"

Muriel Murray's face had gone sheet-white, and her throat was too strangulated for speech.

"Not something the matter, is there, dear?" asked Morris.

15

The Fiend of the Fell

"Honest," said Keith, "we thought you were wonderful. The funniest thing we've ever seen."

"*Funny*," said Willoughby Wellington in a hollow voice. "I recite to you the most moving poem in the English language, and you call it *funny*."

"You'd be a wow on the telly," said Krystle.

"The telly?" asked Wellington. "And what, pray, is the telly?"

They told him about television. And Boot, who had been banished under the bed by Wellington as a punishment for spoiling *The Crossing-Sweeper's Christmas*, crept out to listen, and his eyes widened.

"Hm," said Wellington, when they had finished, "it sounds a mighty thing. Do you mean that *I* could be seen by *everyone*, up and down the kingdom? An audience not of hundreds but . . . *millions*?"

"That's right," said Keith.

"What a marvel!" cried Wellington. "And tell me what great dramatic performances you may see by means of this splendid device? Is Shakespeare to be viewed nightly?"

"Not on your life," said Krystle. "There's pop

videos and soap operas and cartoons and adverts. The adverts are the best."

Wellington repeated these unfamiliar words as if they were lines from *Hamlet*: "Pop videos and soap operas and cartoons and adverts . . . I cannot imagine what these might be. Would you, my friends, bring me one of these machines so that I may see for myself?"

Krystle and Keith looked at each other. "It'd be easier if you came out of the theatre to see one," said Keith. "There's lots in the shops."

At this, Wellington rose to his feet, and began to pace up and down the wardrobe. "I have not been outside this theatre," he said solemnly, "since the night of the coronation of His Majesty, King George the Fifth. And that was in nineteen hundred and ten."

"Eighty years ago," said Keith.

"Is His Majesty still in good health?" enquired Wellington.

"I think he died a long time ago," said Keith.

"Ah," said Wellington, and for a while he walked up and down, saying nothing else.

Keith and Krystle looked at each other, and at Boot, who was peering out from under the bed. Boot winked at them.

"He died, did he?" said Wellington after a long while, still pacing up and down. "My friend and I have a slight problem of that sort. You see— "

At this moment Krystle gave a sudden shriek. A huge rat was running across the floor within a few inches of her feet. Boot made a grab for it, caught it, and began to stroke it. But Wellington had been startled by the shriek, and he dematerialised.

The children looked around, but there was absolutely no sign of him. They looked at Boot, who shrugged, and went on stroking the rat, which seemed to be quite friendly with him.

"You see," said Wellington's voice from nowhere, making the children jump, "my friend and I are not altogether . . . how shall I put it? . . . *solid*."

"You mean you're ghosts," said Krystle.

"Ah," said Wellington's voice. "So you know?" Slowly he materialised again in front of them.

"Oh yes, we know that," said Keith. "It's very exciting. We've never seen ghosts before."

A frown crossed Wellington's face. "I fear," he said gloomily, "that you did not seek me out because of my great reputation as an interpreter of Shakespeare, but merely because I am . . . " and his voice began to break into a sob, "a common . . . *ghost*." He sank down on a chair, burying his face melodramatically in his hands.

At this, Boot sprang up from beneath the bed, grabbed an old dust-sheet, threw it over his head, and began to prance about the wardrobe like a child playing at ghosts.

"Stop it!" thundered Wellington. "Is this to be the pathetic end to my great career? Incarcerated with a miserable buffoon, and sought out by children as a comic curiosity? *Funny*," he went on, in the bitterest of voices. "A *funny* ghost."

"Dunno what you're fussing about," said Krystle. "You could make a fortune. You could be really famous. World famous."

Wellington glanced up sharply at her. "Famous

. . . as a *ghost*?" he said, as bitterly as before. "What sort of fame is that?"

"Better than sitting around here by yourselves, I'd have thought," said Keith. "Anyway, even if you became famous as a ghost rather than an actor, you could still act to people, and show them how good you are."

"Listen," said Krystle, in tones that sounded very like her father describing some new money-making project, "the world is full of actors, see? It's not full of ghosts, see? Or if it is, no one ever sees 'em. Get out there, and you'd be in all the papers, on all the telly shows. You'd make a fortune. See?"

Boot nodded enthusiastically, to show how much he liked the idea, but Wellington would only say, "Hm," and look thoughtful.

"The thing we need to know," said Krystle, "is whether you can do the ghost thing real good."

"The ghost thing?" asked Wellington, puzzled. "Whatever do you mean, child?"

"Oh, come on," said Krystle, "you know. Appearing and disappearing, and carrying your head under your arm, and walking through walls and things. Bet you can't."

Wellington looked at her thoughtfully, then nodded slowly. "I believe," he said, "I know the very thing you have in mind." He went over to Boot and whispered in his ear. Then he motioned to the children to wait while he got ready. He retired behind the curtain.

Boot ran about the wardrobe, busying himself with preparations. He hung an old piece of curtain over the window and brought out an oil lamp, which he placed in the centre of the floor and lit. He handed several items of clothing to Wellington behind the curtain and then put a record on the gramophone – eerie, sinister music.

Suddenly an enormous voice boomed out of nowhere, just behind Krystle's and Keith's ears. *"You are about to meet your doom!"* it thundered, making them jump. Even Boot scuttled for safety underneath the bed. *"You are about to encounter* THE FIEND OF THE FELL!"

There was a flash and a puff of smoke – from some old flash-powder left over from the theatre's pantomimes years ago – and *something began to come up through the floor*.

It was very black, and though it had a human shape, there seemed to be no face. Gradually they realised that it was a figure in a black cloak and hood. Slowly it rose, until the whole creature was standing on the floor. Keith and Krystle shrank back, cowering as far away from it as they could get.

And now the creature cast back its hood, and began to glare at them. Its eyes were bright green, and they flashed terribly. It had long vampire teeth, which it gnashed horribly. It waved its arms at them, and they saw that at the end of its fingers were terrible claw-like nails.

Krystle began to laugh.

There was no getting away from it: the creature was really terribly funny, especially as they knew it was Wellington, acting for all he was worth. The flashing green eyes and the vampire teeth and the claws looked like something out of a rather tatty ghost train at a fair. Certainly it was clever of Wellington to have come through the floor, but now that he had arrived, they couldn't help laughing.

Keith was soon laughing as helplessly as Krystle. As for Boot, his silent laughter was uncontrollable.

He had crawled out from under the bed, and was heaving and spluttering with laughs. He staggered to his feet, and threw himself on the bed as he laughed. And then something quite extraordinary happened.

Boot came to pieces.

It began with his head floating off – still laughing. It floated up to the ceiling, tears of laughter running down its cheeks. Then the arms and legs detached themselves, and scattered into the air all around the wardrobe. And each piece of him was heaving and shaking with laughter.

"Wow," said Keith.

"That really *is* something," said Krystle.

16

Shopping Expedition

Back at Crawley Castle, J.C.B. was on the telephone to the residence of a rich banker whom he knew didn't mind being disturbed at weekends, if there was money in it.

"Guess what, Archie ol' son," he was telling the banker, "I've come into a theatre . . . 'Course, there's money in it," he went on, puffing on a very large cigar. "How much? Enough to make both of us fortunes," he went on sweetly. "So, if you can lay yer paws on, say, the odd thirty mill right away, then *we* could be partners in Europe's first – and I do mean *first* – themed theatrical shopping centre or retail development."

The banker thought about the idea, and agreed that it could make their fortunes. He also agreed to meet J.C.B. at the Theatre Royal, first thing Monday morning.

Back at the theatre, Wellington had vanished – desperately offended that Krystle and Keith had laughed at the Fiend of the Fell. As for Boot, the children were trying to put him together again. It was very difficult, because the pieces of him that had floated away were like smoke to the touch – if you tried to grasp hold of them, your fingers went right through them. The only way to move them was to fan them gently, or blow at them. Then, like smoke rings, they would go where you wanted.

At last all the pieces were in the right place, and Boot got up and walked around to show them he was back to normal. "Where's Mr Wellington?" they asked him anxiously. He shrugged his shoulders. Then he ran over to the window and pointed out at the town, looking at them hopefully.

"I think he wants to go out there and see the shops," said Krystle. Boot nodded energetically.

"It's too late today," said Keith. "And tomorrow's Sunday. They'll be closed. What about Monday morning?"

Boot nodded enthusiastically.

"Okay," said Krystle. "See you here first thing Monday morning."

At 17 Cherrytree Close it was a difficult weekend. Muriel was furious with Keith for having disappeared in the town for so long, and as she was so angry Keith couldn't tell her where he'd been. Also, she was in a dreadful temper with Morris, though Keith couldn't make out why. He was thoroughly glad when it was Monday morning.

Wondering how he could get to the theatre this time, Keith had decided to tell his mum he was meeting Krystle to "practise some ballet". He guessed Muriel would be so pleased that he and Krystle liked each other she wouldn't complain. He was right. "Quite the little ballet stars you'll be soon," cooed Muriel. Keith bit his lip and said nothing.

Krystle was waiting outside the theatre. Without

saying a word, they pushed the stage door open – and jumped with surprise, for Wellington and Boot were waiting for them just inside. Boot was holding a tattered umbrella, and Wellington was wearing a travelling cape and tall hat that made him seem like something out of Sherlock Holmes.

Wellington was still looking very offended that they had laughed at the Fiend of the Fell, and said nothing, merely bowing slightly by way of greeting. Boot grinned and waved his umbrella in the air.

"Out we go, then," smiled Krystle. "Out we go into wonderful Wibberley-on-the-Wold, the crummiest town in England!"

"Don't tell 'em that," said Keith. "Let them make up their own minds. You never know – they might love it!"

At first they did. Both ghosts stood amazed at the sight of the main road, with cars whizzing past, and huge new buildings towering up all around them. Boot jumped up and down with excitement, and Wellington spread his arms wide and breathed in the air deeply. "What a grand place!" he exclaimed. "Can you imagine how joyful it is, after eighty years of confinement, to taste the air of freedom?"

At that moment a lorry went past, belching black fumes from its exhaust pipe. Wellington got a mouthful of them, and began to cough and choke.

But the real trouble didn't begin until they reached the big street outside the shopping centre. Wibberly Town Council had decreed that this street should be "pedestrianised", that is, no cars or lorries were to drive along it. But they let buses use it. This meant that you could be walking down the centre of the street and suddenly find a bus a few inches behind you.

Sure enough, just as the children were crossing this street with the ghosts, a bus roared up. Krystle, Keith and Wellington dodged out of the way, but Boot was not so nimble. He stood there, amazed by the sight of the huge double-decker bus, and in a moment the bus had knocked him down and run him over.

"Oh no!" gasped Keith.

"Shouldn't worry," said Krystle. "He's just come to pieces again, that's all." Sure enough, Boot's head, arms, legs and body were bouncing around the street, each going its own way. It would be a dreadful bother to get them all together again, especially if they didn't want to attract people's attention to the ghosts.

Wellington didn't seem to realise that Boot hadn't been killed. Snatching up Boot's umbrella, which was lying in the middle of the road, he rushed after the bus and banged angrily on the driver's window, roaring and shouting in fury. People all along the street stopped to stare – not least because of Wellington's strange clothes.

The bus driver, who hadn't noticed that he'd knocked down anyone, thought he was being threatened by a lunatic, and stopped the bus, got out of his cab and ran to fetch the policeman who was standing at the next street corner. When he and the policeman returned, Wellington was still jumping up and down furiously, but when the policeman stepped forward and took out his notebook, Wellington took fright, and dematerialised.

"Cripes," said the bus driver, turning pale. "Did you see that? He just *vanished*."

The policeman, who had turned pale too, looked

up and down the road for any sign of Wellington, but of course there was none. "Sort of thing you see on the telly," he muttered to himself, before putting his notebook away and going back to his street corner.

By the time that Krystle and Keith had managed to put Boot together, Wellington had reappeared, and the four of them went into the Crawley Centre.

"I reckoned they might like something to eat," said Krystle, "so I pinched some dosh from my dad." She led all four of them into the Merrie Muncher burger bar.

"Most kind, my dear child," said Wellington when he learned of Krystle's intentions. "But I fear that we . . . ahem . . . *ghosts*," (he said the word as if he still found it distasteful), "are not able to digest solid food."

"Oh," said Krystle, disappointed. "Well, Keith and I fancy something, don't we, Keith?"

Keith thought it was rude to eat if the ghosts couldn't, but before he could stop her, Krystle had ordered two cheeseburgers with French fries and a couple of fizzy drinks. He helped her carry the food to the table.

Boot was looking at it hungrily and thirstily, and as Keith sipped his drink, Boot's eyes became pleading. "Couldn't he just have a little?" Keith asked.

Wellington shrugged. "What that person does is his business," he said carelessly. "I shall simply shut my eyes." And he did so.

Boot took the paper cup gratefully – it was a large-size one – and drank a mouthful, rolling it around his tongue. His eyes sparkled with delight.

93

Before Keith could stop him, he had drained the entire drink. He belched happily.

"It doesn't seem to have done him any harm," said Keith.

"Look," said Krystle.

A puddle was spreading on the floor at Boot's feet. "He's wetting himself," Krystle said.

"No he's not," Keith said. "Not like that. It's just going straight through him. Well, it's bound to, isn't it, seeing as he's not really there? But look, something's happened to it."

Certainly the puddle on the floor didn't look like a drink. It had spread into several different streams. One was black as ink. One was white and fizzy. Another was green, and gave off nasty smoke. "It looks like the stuff they give you in chemistry at school," said Keith.

"If you ask me," said Krystle, "the drink is breaking down into all the things they make it out of. Yuck, how nasty. I don't want to finish mine."

A cleaner came past and swabbed up the mess Boot had made.

"I knew it would be embarrassing," muttered Wellington. "Is it over?"

"Yes," said Keith.

But it wasn't over. It had only just begun.

Having finished his drink, Boot was glancing greedily at Krystle and Keith's burgers and chips. And while they were apologising to the cleaner, he made a grab. He crammed both the burgers and all the chips into his mouth.

"Oh no!" said Keith when he saw. "What's going to happen now?"

"I shudder to think, laddie," groaned Wellington.

What happened was that Boot finished his meal with several dollops of tomato ketchup, which he squeezed from the bottle straight into his mouth. Then he burped happily and sat back with his hands folded over his stomach.

Then there was a clanking noise.

Keith looked down. On the floor, by Boot's trousers, a large tin had appeared. It was labelled "Dog food, economy size. Not for consumption by humans". "Where did that come from?" he said to Krystle.

There was another clank, and another tin appeared from nowhere, by Boot's foot. This one was labelled "Potato substitute. Contains flavourings E 12345, E 67890, and E 54321. Not to be eaten in large quantities".

"Are you thinking what I'm thinking?" said Krystle.

Keith nodded. "That's what the burgers and chips are really made of."

There was another clank, and this time a box appeared. It was labelled "Dehydrated cardboard. Just add water to make buns".

"What on earth is that?" asked Keith.

"Obvious," said Krystle. "It's what they make the burger buns out of. I always thought they tasted of cardboard."

They showed Boot what he had done – showed him that by eating the burgers and chips he had turned them back into the things they were made out of. After that there was no holding him back.

He rushed around the Merrie Muncher, grabbing hold of customers' food and drink, and swallowing it. In a few moments the floor of the burger bar was awash with sinister foaming liquids of many colours, while everywhere, with a clanking noise, there kept appearing tins of dog food, potato substitute, and dehydrated cardboard. The customers screamed at this wild apparition, and someone called the police.

"Quick!" said Keith. "Out of here!" The four of them fled before the police could arrive.

The next shop was called "Homely Homes", and was crammed full of furniture. "All you need for an executive lifestyle", boasted the window display.

"Usual cheap rubbish," observed Krystle.

"At least Boot can't do much in here," said Keith.

"That's what you think," said Krystle. "Look, he's started already."

Boot had been delighted to spot all the comfy beds that were displayed in the shop – delighted because for the last eighty years he had had to sleep *under* a bed rather than in it. Here at last was his chance to get into bed and have a really nice sleep.

He got into it, shut his eyes and began to snore loudly.

But a shop manager had already noticed him and ran over. "I'm sorry, sir," he said, "but customers aren't allowed to do that. Out you get."

Boot, however, was now fast asleep and nothing would wake him. The manager fetched an assistant and together they tried to lift Boot. But of course, as he was a ghost their hands went straight through him. By the time they had got over their astonishment, Boot had woken and run over to another part of the shop.

The manager and assistant chased after him, but they still couldn't grab him. He climbed on to a table and stuck out his tongue at them. The manager jumped on to the table after him – whereupon it fell to pieces under the weight (the manager's, not Boot's, who was weightless), and the manager was thrown to the floor.

"Absolute junk, this furniture," said Krystle. "Falls to pieces the moment you touch it. I should know. My dad fills his rotten Crawleyhomes with the stuff."

On and on went the chase, with bedside tables, wardrobes and armchairs collapsing in pieces as the manager scrambled over them in his hopeless attempt to catch Boot. Soon the shop lay in ruins.

"Serve 'em right," said Krystle. "It's no better than the burgers. But let's get out quick." She hurried Wellington and Keith out of the shop – Boot had temporarily vanished, but he rejoined them when they were out of sight of the manager. "Brilliant," said Krystle. "Where next?"

"The TV shop's next door," said Keith. "Surely he can't do much in there?"

But he was wrong.

The moment Wellington saw the TV screens in the window, he cried, "That's it! I recognise the marvellous invention from your description. How does one climb into it, laddie?"

And in a moment, before they could stop him, he had rushed into the shop and somehow climbed into one of the television sets.

Exactly how he did it, they couldn't say. He seemed to melt into the set, through the side, and as he did so, the picture on its screen (of a newsreader) gave way to Wellington's head, very close to the glass, so that it looked huge.

The odd thing was, though he had only climbed

into one set, his picture could be seen on every TV set in the shop.

He peered out of a dozen screens at once, looked round him, then cleared his throat, and began to recite the famous speech of wicked King Richard:

Now is the winter of our discontent
Made glorious summer by this sun of York . . .

He wasn't wearing the proper costume for the part – the hooked rubber nose, and the false hump, not to mention the long snaky black wig – but it was still pretty frightening. Everyone in the shop stopped and stared, and an assistant started fiddling with one of the sets.

"Funny," he said. "They shouldn't all be showing the same picture."

But they were, and no amount of altering the controls could get rid of Wellington's face.

Meanwhile Boot had gone mad. There was no other word for it.

It had started as soon as he heard the pop music on the radios in the shop. He began jigging wildly up and down – so wildly that Keith expected him to come to pieces at any moment. Then, like Wellington, he somehow managed to affect all the machines at once, all the radios and record players that were booming out the music. It all seemed to get wilder and faster and more noisy as he danced and jigged to it, and soon he was just a crazy blur of arms and legs. Quite a crowd had gathered by now, and Keith could see the police at the back trying to elbow their way to the front to discover what was going on.

In the television sets, Wellington's face had grown bigger and bigger, and ever more snarling and sinister, until suddenly there was an electrical flash, and the sets all went dark. Wellington's face disappeared.

"I think he's bust something," said Krystle.

The police had reached the front of the crowd now. They made a grab at Boot. But he was too quick for them.

He reached up for a satellite TV dish which hung on the wall, spun it so that it began to revolve like a flying saucer, and, as it floated in mid-air, climbed into it. Being merely a ghost, he was light enough for it to hold him, and, as the children watched, the dish carried him out of the shop doorway, past the gaping crowd and the amazed policemen, and down the main arcade of the Crawley Centre, out into the streets beyond.

The police were rooted to the spot with astonishment, but Krystle and Keith ran after him. They realised that Wellington was running alongside them. His face and hair looked a little singed, but he seemed none the worse for wear.

As they watched, Boot zoomed up into the sky on his satellite dish, over the Crawley Centre, and out of sight. People stopped and stared, and one or two even cheered. Keith sighed, and said, "I do hope he's safe on that thing."

"Never mind safe," said Krystle. "He's happy."

"With a bit of luck," said Wellington, "it will carry him far, far away, and I shall never have to see him again. But I do hope he's all right," he added anxiously.

17

A Theatre in the Family

"What was it like inside the television?" Keith asked Wellington as they walked back to the theatre.

"Hot, laddie, hot. Give me the footlights, the grease-paint and the canvas. That's good enough for me. None of this modern stuff."

"You should reopen the theatre," said Krystle.

Wellington smiled. "You think the audiences would come, my dear?"

"If you gave them stuff like today," said Krystle, "They'd come from all over the world. No joking."

"Ah," said Wellington dreamily, "what a wonderful thing it would be if we *did* reopen. I can see it now."

And so he could. The entire theatre restored to its former splendour – red plush seats for the audience, the arch around the stage made bright again with new gold paint, dark red velvet curtains hanging in the glow of the footlights, an orchestra in their stiff white shirts and black evening suits tuning expectantly in the pit, and outside, in lettering six feet high that flashed on and off, lighting up the night sky, his own name.

He described this dream to Keith and Krystle.

"And you could invite lots of other famous actors

here too, couldn't you?" said Keith eagerly. "So that the crowds would flock to see them all?"

Wellington thought about this carefully. "No," he said. "I wouldn't. To be honest, I cannot think of any other member of my profession who would be *quite* good enough to tread the boards with *me*, dear boy."

"Well, here we are, home again."

"Mmm," said Krystle, "but I don't remember leaving the stage door open."

"Perhaps Boot's back already," said Keith.

He was. They found him waiting for them just inside the door. But he looked very worried. Putting his finger to his lips, he took them to the doorway leading on to the stage. They could hear voices.

Krystle and Keith peeped through. Down where the audience sat, a cloud of cigar smoke cleared to reveal the shape of J.C.B. He was talking to a fat little man in an expensive suit.

They couldn't hear a word of what was being said, but there was a lot of waving of arms and pointing to bits of the theatre around them.

"I don't like the look of this," said Krystle in Keith's ear. "I've got a feeling he's gone and bought the old place."

"Great," whispered Keith. "That's just what we want. Now maybe he'll do it up and reopen it like we said."

Krystle gave him a withering look. "Not my old dad. Every place he's ever got hold of in this crummy town, he's knocked down and put up some even crummier new building." She turned to the ghosts. "Stay outa sight," she whispered to them. "And not only that, if

101

you can lock your door upstairs, then do. That way, he can't get at your stuff. Right?"

Boot nodded enthusiastically.

"Leave it to me," whispered Krystle, taking charge. "I'll find out what Dad's up to and then let you know what's what."

"What shall I do?" asked Keith, feeling a bit left out.

"Push off."

"Why should I?" hissed Keith indignantly.

"Just do as I say. I'll phone your house when I've got anything to report."

So they parted, Wellington and Boot going silently upstairs to the wardrobe. Keith went off to get a bus, and Krystle hung about the stage door to talk to J.C.B. as soon as he had finished with the man.

That evening the telephone rang at 17 Cherrytree Close. Keith rushed for it. "It's probably for me," he shouted.

"Might be someone about the gnomes," said Morris hopefully. Muriel said nothing. She still wasn't talking to him.

It was Krystle for Keith. "Bad news," she said. "Not quite as bad as it might have been, but pretty bad."

"What d'you mean?" Keith asked.

"He doesn't want to knock the theatre down, but he wants to turn it into a shopping centre."

"What!" screamed Keith.

"He bought it a couple of days ago – and this is the bit I don't believe. He says he bought it from your dad, for a hundred quid."

"My dad!?"

"That's what he says. Anyway, the builders will

be moving in right away. They'll be ripping out all the old woodwork and everything, and turning it into a crummy *supermarket*, can you believe it?"

"They can't!" yelled Keith.

"Oh yes they jolly well can," Krystle shouted back. "But what are we gonna do about the ghosts? Does your dad know about *them*?"

"Course not, Dumbo. But he does know there was something funny going on in his crummy Crawley Centre today. Everyone knows about that. Haven't you seen? It's all over the front page of tonight's paper:

STRANGE GOINGS ON IN WIBBERLEY SHOPPING CENTRE SHOPS VANDALISED BY GHOSTLY FIGURE. "WHEN I TOUCHED HIM THERE WAS NOTHING THERE" SAYS MANAGER.

"So where are Wellington and Boot now?"

"Still at the theatre, I suppose," said Krystle. "Dad says there's a room at the top of the stairs which is locked, and he hasn't seen inside. That's the wardrobe of course. But his workmen will break the door down, and then where will the ghosts be able to live?"

"Maybe we could find them another theatre," suggested Keith.

"Don't be a dipstick. There isn't one within fifty miles."

"Well, what else do you suggest?" asked Keith, aggrieved.

"*I* suggest," said Krystle, "that you get down there first thing in the morning, right?"

"And what'll you be doing?"

"Working on things at home, of course," she snapped. "There is one good bit of news, though."

"Yeah?" asked Keith. "And what's that?"

"We've got someone else on our side."

"Who?"

"My mum," said Krystle. "For some reason I haven't quite figured, she reckons it's wrong for Dad to go and ruin a theatre."

"Did you tell her about the ghosts?"

"What do you think I am, a complete wally? But with her *and* me having a go at Dad, who knows, we might be able to manage summink." With which Krystle rang off.

Now Cherie Crawley had always dreamed of becoming an actress, ever since she won the Miss Lovely Legs contest. And when Krystle had told her there was an old theatre still standing in Wibberley, and that her very own J.C.B. had bought it, well, Cherie just couldn't conceal her glee.

"But that's simply wunnerful, dahlin'," she purred, clasping her newly-polished stuck-on nails.

"Wot is?" said J.C.B.

"I bet you bought it just so I could tread the boards," went on Cherie. "I got theatrical blood, you know," she went on. She was the daughter of a used-car dealer in Romford, but a great-uncle had once played the back of a pantomime horse for three nights when the regular chap had flu.

"I've bought it, you silly dollop," said J.C.B., "in order to save me bacon. And I intends turnin' it inter Europe's first themed theatrical shoppin' retail whatsit," he added boastfully, blowing a smoke-ring into Cherie's heavily made-up face. "So whaddya think of that, eh?"

"I fink," said Cherie, bursting into tears, "you're a lousy rotten pig."

Things were no better at 17 Cherrytree Close. When Keith asked his dad if it was really true he'd sold the theatre to Krystle's father for a hundred pounds, Muriel burst into tears and said of course it was true. Why she'd married such a fool heaven knows, but she couldn't stand much more of it. With that she went upstairs, packed a suitcase, and went out, slamming the front door.

"She's left us, Dad," said Keith gloomily.

"So she has, son," said Morris. "Still, not to worry. Once I've made me fortune from the gnomes, she'll come running back."

Meanwhile at Crawley Castle, Cherie was still pleading with J.C.B. "Forget it!" he bellowed. "I've got thirty million tied up in this one."

"Brute!" wailed Cherie, and she too went upstairs, packed, and departed, slamming the mock-Jacobean front door behind her.

"Reckon she's left us, Dad," said Krystle.

"Don't worry, Princess," said J.C.B., lighting himself a soothing cigar. "Once I've made that theatre of yours into Europe's most successful themed thingummy, she'll come running back."

And that was how Mrs Cherie Crawley and Mrs Muriel Murray both walked out on their husbands the same evening, and both checked into the Crawley Executive Motor Lodge, which was Wibberley-on-the-Wold's only hotel.

18

A Night at the Hotel

Coincidentally, Wellington and Boot had checked into the hotel too. Or at least they had arrived there and made themselves at home.

Despite the embarrassment caused him by Boot, Wellington had rather enjoyed his trip to the shopping centre. All the people bustling around excited him after years cooped up in the theatre, and though he couldn't decide whether he approved of modern life, he certainly wanted to see more of it.

So when he realised that Krystle's dad had plans for the theatre that would almost certainly make it impossible for him and Boot to continue in their old routine, he decided that they should move out and look for a new home.

The first place to cross his mind, when he considered where they might live, was the Pied Bull Hotel. This was an old coaching inn, and in Victorian times anybody of importance who was visiting Wibberley-on-the-Wold had stayed there. There had been a fine old dining room, where huge joints of meat were carved on trolleys with silver covers; a bar where the richer farmers would gather to drink beer after market, standing in front of a roaring log fire; and good plain bedrooms with brass bedsteads and marble washstands with water-jugs.

"We shall take ourselves to the Pied Bull," Wellington announced to Boot. Boot, who was keen to try anything, nodded enthusiastically.

But when they got there, the Pied Bull had disappeared. Leastways, the original building was still there, but there were a great many new bits, which almost entirely hid the old inn. There was a row of flagpoles outside, with the flags of America, Japan, and several other countries flying from it, and a big sign announcing that it was now the Crawley Executive Motor Lodge.

Wellington and Boot stood and stared. After a while, Wellington shrugged his shoulders. "We may as well see what it's like, laddie," he observed, and together they walked up to the main entrance. Before they got there they dematerialised.

At the reception desk the girl in charge was trying to help a Japanese businessman to book airline tickets, and she didn't notice when two of the room keys – rooms 120 and 121 – unhooked themselves and floated out of the reception area and down the passage to the rooms.

Wellington looked inside both rooms and decided that 121 had the better view. He gave room 120 to Boot.

Five minutes later, Cherie Crawley turned up at the hotel by taxi. She was still in a furious temper with J.C.B. "Gimme a single room," she demanded. "And charge it to my husband's account."

107

"Yes, Mrs Crawley," said the girl, who knew Cherie by sight. "We have a couple of rooms left, 120 and 121, both with en suite bathroom, mini-bar and trouser press. Shall I give you 120?"

Cherie nodded, but when the girl reached for the key it wasn't there. "I expect the last guest didn't return it," she said. "Never mind, I have a spare." And she gave it to Cherie. "Wilf," she called to the porter, "please show Mrs Crawley to room 120."

Two minutes later Muriel Murray arrived at the reception desk. She couldn't afford to take a taxi, and it had been a long walk from Cherrytree Close. She hadn't meant to waste money on a hotel room, but she didn't know where else to go – it was late in the evening – so when she saw the motor lodge she decided to spend the night there while collecting her thoughts.

"We have just the one single room left, madam," said the girl. "It features an en suite bathroom, mini-bar and trouser press."

Then she told Muriel the price.

"Haven't you anything cheaper?" gasped Muriel.

The girl, whose name was Tiffany, and who wore a sophisticated black bow in her hair, looked Muriel up and down, and chose her daintily-pronounced words carefully.

"We would like to remind madam that this is the Crawley Executive Motor Lodge, part of the Crawleyhomes Group. Exclusive executive standards are our specialty. For example, in the en suite bathroom we offer free of charge not only a shower cap and bubble bath, madam, but an absolutely free little sachet of shampoo."

Muriel's mouth fell open.

"And therefore, madam, if madam does not wish to avail herself of such executive standards, but is seeking somewhere cheaper, then why doesn't madam try one of the *crummy bed and breakfasts* down the road? *Goodnight*, madam."

"Give me the key," said Muriel haughtily, wondering how on earth she was going to pay, but refusing to be snubbed like this.

"Yes, madam," said Tiffany. "Oh . . . that one's missing too." So once again a spare had to be found. "Your name, madam?"

"Du Maurier," snapped Muriel.

"Take the lady's bag, Wilf," said Tiffany to the muttering old hall porter, who'd only just puffed down to room 120 with Cherie's load. "She's in room 121. Have a nice stay, Mrs Doomery."

Once he had settled into room 121, Wellington had taken off his shoes, lain down on the bed and fallen fast asleep. But in room 120 Boot remained firmly awake. There were so many things to explore. In the far corner was a cupboard with a notice saying "Mini-bar: please help yourself. All drinks will be charged to your bill".

He picked up a bottle – it happened to be champagne – and shook it very hard. Then he pulled out the cork and let the foaming liquid spray all over the room.

Next he tried the telly, but he soon got bored with all the channels and decided to explore the bathroom. He ran himself an enormous bath, poured in all the little bottles of shampoo and bubble bath that he found

109

on the ledge, threw off all his clothes (leaving them on the bedroom floor) and plunged into the steaming hot water.

It was at this moment that Cherie Crawley came into the bedroom. Hearing a noise, Boot immediately dematerialised. Invisible, he lay in the bath.

Cherie looked around her, and was horrified by the mess. Old clothes lay all over the floor, someone seemed to have sprayed champagne everywhere, and the room was in chaos. Also, somebody had recently been having a bath. There were still clouds of steam in the bathroom, and the bath was full of water.

Angrily, Cherie rang the reception desk and demanded that a cleaner be sent to clear up the mess at once.

Meanwhile Wellington, asleep on his bed, was woken by the sound of *his* door opening. At once he jumped up and ran into the bathroom to hide.

Muriel looked round the room and had the odd feeling that someone else had been in there just a moment ago. There were creases on the bed, as if a person had been lying there, and the bathroom door was open. She pushed it shut and straightened the bedcover.

Next door, in number 120, the cleaner had tidied up the room, carrying away the old clothes to put in the dustbin. Cherie decided that now everything was clean she would have a bath herself.

Boot, meanwhile, had climbed out of the bath and was standing invisibly in a corner of the bedroom, wondering how he could get his clothes back.

Cherie took off her dress and went into the bathroom, shutting the door. Boot looked at the dress and decided to get his own back on this tiresome woman who had had his clothes removed. He put on the dress.

Cherie was just about to get into the bath when she remembered she had left the Crawley crown jewels (as J.C.B. called her diamond rings and necklaces) in the bedroom. And he'd told her never to let them out of her sight. So she came out of the bathroom in her underwear to fetch them.

She stopped and stared with amazement. Her dress, with no one inside it, was dancing on the bed all by itself.

Cherie screamed and made a grab for the Crawley crown jewels.

The dress gave a yell and made a beeline for the door.

Hearing the noise, Muriel came out of her room. She was amazed to see Cherie Crawley standing in the doorway of her room, in her underwear, shaking like a leaf.

"Why, it's Mrs Crawley, isn't it?" she said. "Whatever is the matter?"

"It's my room," gasped Cherie. "It's haunted!"

"You just come into mine, dear," said Muriel soothingly. "I've got a mini-bar in mine," she added grandly.

Cherie followed her into room 121, and sat down, while Muriel proudly fussed around with her mini-bar and poured them both a drink.

Wellington, meanwhile, was watching both ladies through a crack in the bathroom door. This was not at all the peaceful night in a hostelry he had been looking forward to. He therefore decided to get rid of the intruders as quickly as possible.

"Ooh, it was just terrifying, I can't tell you, Moor-ree-yell," Cherie was saying (this was how she pronounced "Muriel").

"Ooh, it must have been," said Muriel.

There was a low moaning sound from the bathroom. Cherie and Muriel froze. "W-w-w-what was that?" said Muriel.

"You don't fink, Moor-ree-yell," said Cherie, "that *your* room could be haunted too?"

"Stuff and nonsense," said Muriel. "It may come complete with mini-bar and trouser press, but no one said anything about an en suite . . . *ghost!*" she ended on a scream.

For the bathroom door had swung open to reveal Willoughby Wellington as the Fiend of the Fell – wearing the Crawley Executive Motor Lodge bathrobe and free shower cap for extra effect.

He had never had a more receptive audience. Cherie and Muriel screamed their heads off.

19

Conference at the Castle

At Crawley Castle, J.C.B. was spending the evening thinking up a name for the new shopping centre. "The Prestige Executive Themed Theatre," he muttered to himself, lighting a cigar. "The Theatre Royal Retail Development. The Theatre Shop. Shopping at the Theatre . . . " He was beginning to doze off when he heard a commotion outside the window. He looked out. Cherie had just arrived in a taxi with some other woman – her face was familiar – and they both seemed to be in a terrible state. Sighing, J.C.B. went to the main door to see what was going on.

Meanwhile Morris, too, had set out for Crawley Castle in the Maxi. When Muriel had walked out on him, he'd sat thinking for a while. After a good deal of mental effort he came to this conclusion, "I think it was me sellin' that theatre wot upset her."

"Got it in one, Dad," said Keith.

"D'you reckon if I saw that Crawley chap and offered him his hundred quid, he'd let me have the theatre back again?"

"Who can say?" shrugged Keith, though privately he didn't give the scheme one chance in a thousand.

So off they went, with Morris packing another box of gnomes in the untidy back of the Maxi as an afterthought – "You never know when they may come in handy, son."

To get to Crawley Castle they had to pass through the centre of Wibberley. They were waiting at the traffic lights just by the Crawley Executive Motor Lodge when one of the car rear doors seemed to open and shut by itself. Keith turned round, but he couldn't see anything. Morris didn't appear to have noticed the noise.

The door had in fact been opened by Boot, and he and Wellington, both dematerialised, had got into the car while it was waiting at the lights.

Boot had managed to find his own clothes in the hotel dustbins, and he and Wellington had decided to get away from the Motor Lodge and find somewhere quieter to spend the night. It was Boot who had spotted Keith in the back of the Maxi, and before Wellington could stop him, he had opened the door and climbed into the car. Wellington decided to join him.

All the way to Crawley Castle, Keith had the sensation that someone was sitting in the back of the car, and he kept glancing over his shoulder. Then, just as they were drawing up at the main door of the castle, he heard Wellington whisper in his ear, "It's us, laddie!"

"The ghosts!" said Keith delightedly.

"Whassat?" said Morris.

"You probably won't believe this, Dad," said Keith, "but there's a couple of ghosts travelling in the back of this car."

Morris spun round and looked over his shoulder, but of course he saw nothing. And he wasn't looking where he was going. There was a *crunch* as the Maxi bumped heavily into the back of the white Rolls, JCB 2, that was parked outside the main door of the Castle. And a second *crunch* as this Rolls, pushed forward by the impact, ran into the back of the other white Rolls, JCB 1, which was parked just in front of it.

"I don't believe it!" shouted J.C.B., jumping up and down with rage on the doorstep. "Both me flaming cars at once – and both of 'em only just back from the repairers. I'll have your guts for sausages!" he yelled to Morris.

Krystle came out to see what all the noise was about. "Oh, it's you," she said to Keith. "I see your dad's gone and done it again."

"It was when I told him about the ghosts," said Keith.

"Ghosts?" yelled J.C.B. "Why does everyone keep goin' on about flamin' ghosts? First it's a ghost in me shoppin' centre. Then it's ghosts in me 'otel. And now it's flamin' ghosts 'ere! Once and for all, *there are no such things as flamin' ghosts!*"

"Oh yes there are, Dad," said Krystle. "So why don't we all just go inside, and then everyone can hear the whole story."

So a few moments later they were all sitting in the master lounge of Crawley Castle, while Keith and Krystle explained all about Wellington and Boot to an audience of J.C.B., Cherie, Muriel and Morris.

"Nice one, Princess," said J.C.B. to Krystle when they had finished. "You could be a script-writer on the telly one day."

115

Krystle wrinkled up her nose in disgust. "You don't believe us, do you?" she said.

"I'd like to darlin'," said J.C.B. "But like your old Daddy said before, THERE ARE NO SUCH THINGS AS GHOSTS."

"Oh yes there are," said Keith, pointing at the door. "Look!"

The door of the master lounge had opened of its own accord, and into the room were dancing four little creatures. Two carried spades over their shoulders, and the other two had fishing rods.

"I thought you said they was ghosts," squealed Cherie. "This lot look more like— "

"Garden gnomes," said Morris proudly. "Clever little chaps – I had no idea they could get about under their own steam like that. And as it happens, I am sole agent for these gnomes in this part of Great Britain. They're available at knock-down prices— "

"Don't be an ass, Dad," interrupted Keith. "Can't you see they're not moving by themselves? Someone's holding them."

"Oh," said Morris, crestfallen. And at that moment, Wellington and Boot became visible.

They looked a little sheepish at having come into Crawely Castle uninvited, but they put down the gnomes, and allowed Keith and Krystle to introduce them to everyone.

"Mr Willoughby Wellington, the great Shakespearean tragic actor," said Keith. Wellington smiled happily, and bowed deeply to everyone.

"And Bert Boot, the funniest clown since – or should that be before? – Charlie Chaplin," said Krystle. Wellington looked offended, but Boot grinned and accepted the glass of champagne that J.C.B. offered him.

"Are you sure you should?" said Keith, remembering what had happened in the Merrie Muncher, but Boot nodded enthusiastically and drank the champagne at one gulp.

There was a clanking noise, and on the floor next to Boot's trousers appeared a bottle labelled "British cooking wine mixed with fizzy lemonade".

Krystle laughed. "Always thought you got that champagne pretty cheap, eh, Dad?"

J.C.B. looked gobsmacked.

"Well, say something then, Dad," said Krystle, who was loving every minute of her dad's discomfort.

"Er . . . Welcome to Crawley Castle, gents!" said J.C.B. to the ghosts. "And to the start of what could prove to be a brilliant new business relationship," he added cryptically.

"Why, thank you," said Wellington, bowing. "And maybe I might be permitted to celebrate the occasion by organising a small dramatic entertainment with my young friends here?"

"Feel free," said J.C.B., lighting another cigar and offering the box to Welllington and Boot.

"Not for me, thank you," said Wellington, but Boot took one and lit it, and coughed so much that he came to pieces. It took Keith and Krystle several minutes to round up all the bits and put them together again. Then they and Wellington and Boot had a brief whispered discussion, after which Wellington stepped forward and announced to the grown-ups, "The company of the Theatre Royal, Wibberley-on-the-Wold,

117

starring Mr Willoughby Wellington, also featuring Mr
Bert Boot, and introducing Miss Krystle Crawley and
Mr Keith Murray— "

"Du Maurier," said Muriel.

" —are proud to present a special performance, for
one night only, of *The Theatre Saved*, a melodrama of
old and new Wibberley. Lights! Music!"

Keith, standing by the lightswitch, dimmed the
lighting, and Krystle put a compact disc on her dad's
machine – heavy thudding rock music, which was the
only kind of record he had.

Wellington began to speak over the music:

> In olden days of great renown,
> Our Wibberley was a fine old town,
> With coaching inn and honest folk.
> The plain old English tongue they spoke,
> And in their plain old shops they bought
> What they did need, of honest sort.
> Among their buildings, very grand,
> The theatre, finest in the land,
> Where honest actors jerked a tear,
> And sang a song, and shook a spear.

"Good old Shakespeare," muttered Krystle.
Wellington gave her an approving smile. Then
he went on:

> But then the theatre shut its doors;
> No more applause, no more encores!
> The stage, where strutted kings and fools,
> Is now the haunt of ghosts and ghouls.

At this, Keith switched out the lights entirely, and Krystle raised the level of the music. Wellington vanished. There was a pause. Then, slowly, a green shimmering shape began to come up through the floor.

Muriel screamed, but Morris said: "Nothing to be frightened of, love. It's all done with them laser lights, like they have in the discos."

Slowly, the Fiend of the Fell rose through the floor, flashing his eyes. Then he floated slowly across the room, bared his vampire teeth at the onlookers, and, with a terrible shriek, vanished through the wall of the master lounge.

Everyone gasped, but there were more remarkable things to come. Suddenly, from nowhere, a ball bounced across the floor. Then it stopped, and opened its eyes. It was a head. A luminous green head. The head grinned at the audience, and Muriel screamed again.

"It's all trick stuff really," said Morris. "There's a fellow out the back there pulling wires."

Hearing this, the head bounced into Morris's lap, and sat there, grinning horribly at him. Even Morris began to look a bit disturbed at this.

Next, a green shimmering hand rose out of a flower-vase on the table, and waved. Another hand came out of a picture on the wall, and shook its fist at everyone. A leg emerged from the television set, and kicked itself about. Finally, the other leg came out of J.C.B.'s cigar box. After this, everything went black again.

When the lights came up once more, Keith and Krystle were standing by the table. Krystle spoke first:

119

> Those spectres in the theatre dwell;
> They like their life there very well.

Keith said:

> But now they'll have to leave their home,
> And through the wide, wide world to roam.

Keith and Krystle then said together:

> For them the outlook's very poorly,
> All on account of Mister Crawley.
> So one and all, please hear our groan:
> *Why won't you leave the ghosts alone?*

At which they took a bow, and the ghosts emerged and took a bow with them, and then Wellington, who loved taking bows, took about ten more, and the four members of the audience applauded wildly.

"Told you our Keithie'd make a lovely little performer," said Muriel, proudly nudging her husband.

"And what about my little Princess?" said J.C.B.

"A star in the making," said Muriel.

Morris said, "Clever stuff, but that chap Paul Daniels does it better."

J.C.B. poured more champagne, and said, "Well, I reckon you've made your point, Princess."

"You mean, you agree with us, Dad?" said Krystle.

"Sure thing, Princess. We'd be crazy to throw these wonderful guys out of their home."

"You really think so?" said Keith delightedly.

"Would I be such a flaming idiot?" said J.C.B.

"And what about the theatre?" said Krystle. "Would

120

you let us reopen it, so that Wellington and Boot can perform there again?"

"Would I let you do it?" echoed J.C.B. "Princess, the reopening of the Theatre Royal, Wibberley-on-the-Wold, will be the biggest and most sensational project ever undertaken by Crawleyhomes."

"That's fantastic!" said Keith. He and Krystle and the ghosts began to dance round in a circle, singing, "We're going to reopen the theatre, we're going to reopen the theatre!"

"What'll be your first appearance?" Keith asked Wellington.

"Wicked King Richard was always a crowd-puller," answered Wellington. "But for such an heroic occasion, I think Henry the Fifth should meet the bill."

J.C.B. cleared his throat. "I reckon there's one thing I oughter make clear to you guys. This Shakespeare stuff ain't quite what's wanted in the 1990s."

Wellington stopped in his tracks. "What do you mean?" he asked, in a shaky voice.

"Look at it like this," said J.C.B. "Yer verse-speakin' stuff, all them battles an' that, that's fine for yer fancy National Theatre, an' the Royal Shakespeare, an' things like that, when guys like me ain't payin' the bill. But I gotta see a return on me dosh."

Krystle sighed. "I knew it," she said.

"Daddy has to give the public what it wants, see Princess?" said J.C.B.

"And what does the public want?" asked Wellington hollowly.

"Ghosts," said J.C.B.

"Ghosts?" said Keith.

"Ghosts," repeated J.C.B. "Ghoulies, monsters, vampires, demons, headless horsemen, anything you like, providin' they're *real*. Can't yer see it? The only place in the world what's got *real ghosts* on display. Listen, fellas, it'll make our flamin' fortunes. Like I said, this is gonna be the start of a wunnerful business relationship."

20

The Greatest Show on Earth

J.C.B. always moved fast when he had an idea, and only a few days later the Theatre Royal was abuzz with activity. Workmen were cleaning the place from top to bottom. The front of the building was being restored to its former glory, and everywhere – around the town as well as outside the theatre – signs were going up: "Opening shortly – the fabulously terrifying musical *Spookeasy*, featuring THE WIBBERLEY GHOSTS." Similar announcements were appearing in the national newspapers, and J.C.B. himself was seen in a TV advert in which he promised viewers the greatest show on earth – at Wibberley-on-the-Wold.

"Isn't it good to see the old place looking so smart?" said Keith, as he and Krystle stood outside the theatre, watching the workmen. "Wellington and Boot must be really pleased."

"Dunno about that," said Krystle. "You know Wellington doesn't like being called a ghost. He didn't seem too keen on the idea of giving a performance like something from *Ghostbusters*."

"But think of the money he'll make," said Keith.

"Your dad says it's going to make everyone's fortunes."

"Yeah," said Krystle, "but a fortune's not much use if you're a ghost. I mean, you can't eat or drink, and you don't need half the things we need. Anyway, knowing my dad, the only person who'll make a fortune out of it is *him*."

"He's sure people will flock from all over the country to see the ghosts."

"All over the world," said Krystle. "He's doing deals with airlines for special tickets and things, and he's trying to get the motorway people to finish ahead of schedule so all the rich people can drive from London in their Rollers and Jags and not have any traffic to get stuck in."

"Come on," said Keith. "Let's go and see how the ghosts are."

They went in through the stage door – only to find their way barred by an enormous security man.

"*All security passes must be shown!*" roared the security man.

"We haven't got any," said Krystle.

"Oh dear, oh dear," said the security man, his little piggy eyes lighting up with nasty pleasure.

"Listen, you oaf, I'm a *Crawley!*" squealed Krystle, finding herself dangling at the end of a pair of ape-like arms.

"And I'm *Little Bo Peep!*" boomed the security man.

"Well, I like that!" said Keith, dusting himself down outside. "Who was it who discovered the ghosts in the first place?"

"Typical Dad," said Krystle glumly. "Whenever he gets hold of anything it's always crawling with security people and lawyers and all kinds of idiots with briefcases and portable telephones. Come on, there's a hole in the wall, let's climb through that."

Once they were inside the theatre, so many people were bustling about, giving each other orders and getting in each other's way, that nobody paid any attention to them. There were cables everywhere, and men sawing and drilling and hammering, and huge lights kept coming on and off, and there were bursts of enormously loud music from loudspeakers, and every kind of chaos.

Keith and Krystle found their way to the staircase that led to the wardrobe. Even this had been smartened up. There was fresh paint everywhere, and all the dressing rooms now had names on the door: "Mr J.C.B. Crawley", "Personal Assistant to Mr J.C.B. Crawley", "Mr Crawley's Chief Accountant", and so on.

"You'd have thought they'd have given Wellington and Boot the best dressing rooms," said Keith.

On the top floor, the wardrobe had disappeared. At least, the room itself was still there, but all the old costumes had been cleared out, and a notice on the door said "Artists' Catering and Hospitality". Inside were crates of orange juice and champagne. A man in a white coat with a clipboard was checking items on a list.

"Where's Wellington and Boot?" asked Krystle.

"Never heard of 'em," said the man in the white coat.

"But they're the stars of the show," said Keith. "The Wibberley ghosts."

"Oh, them," said the man in the white coat. "You

mean Ghastly Grimface and the Headless Horror."

"Is that what Dad's calling them?" said Krystle without surprise. "Wellington won't like that."

"So where are they?" asked Keith. "This is their room, you know. They've lived here for eighty years."

"Dunno nothing about that," said the man. "This is 'Catering and Hospitality' now, so clear out. I've got this lot to unpack."

Keith and Krystle cleared out.

Across the street, near where Keith and Krystle had been standing a few minutes earlier, Wellington and Boot, invisible, were watching the workmen cleaning up the theatre.

"Ghastly Grimface," muttered Wellington in his gloomiest voice. "Ghastly Grimface and the Headless Horror. To think a great Shakespearean should stoop so low!"

Boot, who was looking equally gloomy, nodded in agreement.

At first, when J.C.B. proposed his plan, Wellington had quite liked it. The idea of thousands of people – maybe even millions – flocking to Wibberley-on-the-Wold to see *him* was absolutely irresistible. It was only when the workmen arrived at the theatre and turned the whole place upside down that he began to have second thoughts.

J.C.B. had suggested to the ghosts that they come and stay at Crawley Castle while the theatre was being made ready. Wellington had refused at first; he said he would prefer to remain in his old home. But where was that old home now? It had disappeared beneath all the new paint, the cables, the lights, and all the men busily giving each other orders.

So he and Boot had walked out, just before the children arrived. "To the castle, Boot!" said Wellington, and Boot nodded.

An empty taxi had stopped at the traffic lights where they were standing. Boot opened the door and climbed in. Wellington followed him. Both were still invisible, so the driver, turning round, saw the door apparently open and shut by itself.

"Good morning, gentlemen," he said cheerfully. "What an honour this is – I'm privileged to be giving a ride to the Wibberley ghosts."

Wellington and Boot were astonished. Had they failed to dematerialise, and could the driver see them? No, when they looked they saw they were as invisible as ever.

"I know you're there, gentlemen," said the driver, "because I saw that door open and shut, so it must be you! Good morning, gentlemen."

"Good morning," said Wellington, gloomily, becoming visible again. Boot became visible too. He sat there looking just as uncomfortable as Wellington.

"Yes," went on the driver, "I know all about you two! You must be Ghastly Grimface, and that one's the Headless Horror, except that he hasn't taken off his head today. Well, gentlemen, and where can I take you? The ride's free, of course. It's the least I can do, in return for all you're doing for this town."

"To Crawley Castle, if you please," said Wellington. "But what do you mean, my man, about helping the town? What are my friend and I doing for it?"

"Bringing us lots of dosh," said the driver, as he set off for the castle. "Loadsa money. D'you know they're

127

gonna build three new hotels specially to accommodate visitors to your show? And there's loadsa new shops gonna open, gift shops most of 'em, selling models of you two, and records of ghostly noises, an' all that sorta stuff."

"Is that so?" said Wellington.

"Surprised you don't know about it," said the driver. "Course that bloke Crawley's gonna make millions an' millions out of it, but us ordinary folks'll do okay too. Loadsa tourists taking taxi rides, all that sorta thing. Loadsa people going to the gift shops."

"Does this mean," said Wellington thoughtfully, "that, because of us . . . ghosts . . . this town will be spoilt even more?"

"Dunno what you mean by 'spoilt'," said the driver. "I mean, it's a *town* we're talkin' about, right? I mean, I'm all for this conservation stuff, this Green Party an' unleaded petrol an' all that sorta thing, that's all right in the *country*, ain't it? But a town's a town. You gotta make money in a town. An' that means progress."

"I see," said Wellington. "And progress means knocking down fine old buildings and putting up new ones?"

"You got it, squire," said the driver, "you got it in one."

The taxi had halted at the motorway works, because the traffic lights were red. Wellington and Boot looked out of the window, at all the mud and machinery and mess.

"What's this?" said Wellington. "Is this the country?"

128

"Used to be," said the taxi driver. "But they needed it for the motorway."

"And what, pray, is a motorway?" asked Wellington.

"What's a motorway?" repeated the driver, unbelievingly. "Course, I forgot, you bin shut up in that theatre for a hundred years. Well, a motorway is a big road, so's lotsa cars an' lorries can get from one place to another."

"Why should they want to do that?" asked Wellington.

"Well, they gotta do it, ain't they?" said the driver. "I mean, that's what cars an' lorries are for. They come from London an' go to Birmingham, an' soon they'll go from Birmingham to Wibberley."

"And is Birmingham so very different from London? And is Wibberley so very different from Birmingham?" asked Wellington.

The driver thought for a moment. "Not really," he said. "Everywhere's much the same nowadays."

"So why cannot all these cars and lorries stay in the same place?" asked Wellington.

"Well," said the driver, "now you mention it, I s'pose they could. But that's not the way we goes about things these days. Things is different, see, since your old Victorian times. Like I say, it's progress. Off we go, lights have changed."

And off they went. And Wellington, engrossed in his conversation with the driver, failed to notice that Boot had quietly opened the door of the taxi and slipped off. So that when the taxi arrived at Crawley Castle, there was only one ghost on board.

"What's happened to yer friend?" asked the driver.

129

Wellington shrugged his shoulders. "Thank you for the ride," he said.

"Pleasure, squire. Don't want no money. But do us a favour, take yer 'ead off an' gibber for me, will you? Then I can tell the missus I've really seen one of them Wibberley ghosts."

21

An Alteration in the Plans

When he got out of the taxi, Boot dematerialised
again. Invisibly, he began to wander around the
motorway workings.

He stared at the big earth-moving machines, the
lorries, and the caravans where the workmen slept at
night. He peered into the enormous hole that had been
dug as a quarry for sand and gravel. He looked amazed
at the mess that had been made of the countryside.

The motorway had reached a point where it was
about to cross lonely moorland, the haunt of rare
birds and wild flowers. Boot didn't know this, but
for months the local people had been trying to stop
the Government building the motorway through this
fine stretch of unspoilt land. They had failed, and the
machines and workmen were going to start work on
this stretch the very next day.

Boot climbed up on to one of the big machines, to
get a better view. He could see how the men had
marked the line of the road with posts and string.
He looked behind him, to where the motorway had
already spoilt the countryside as far as the eye could
see. He had heard what the taxi driver had said about

the cars and lorries that would soon roar along this road. And he looked to one side, where in a cluster of trees stood the ugly pile of Crawley Castle.

He sat there, looking, for a long time. Then he climbed down and, still invisible, began to explore the caravans that were ranged along one side of the motorway works.

At the castle, J.C.B. was amazed to see Wellington. "Flippin' heck," he said, "it's Ghastly Grimface. What you done with the other one, the 'Eadless 'Orror?"

Wellington flinched at these names. "My friend has been detained," he answered coldly. "He presents his apologies. No doubt we shall see him later." In fact he hadn't the faintest idea where Boot had gone, or what he was up to. And he didn't care. He wished that Keith and Krystle had never discovered him and Boot in the theatre, and that they'd never got mixed up in all these ghastly money-making plans. In fact he wished that he and Boot had never become ghosts at all, but had died completely and finally eighty years ago, when the theatre shut. Most of all he wished he had never seen the horrible mess that was being made of the world in modern times.

"So you wanna stay here after all, eh?" said J.C.B., lighting another of his cigars. "Well, me ol' fruit, that suits me, 'cos you can be 'ere, at hand, to discuss final arrangements for the opening night, right?"

Wellington cringed.

"Course," went on J.C.B., chomping on his cigar, "there's been lotsa mega-changes to the original plan. Live TV coverage in no less than sixteen countries for a kick-off, ol' fruit. Merchandising and video rights already sold for ten million, lots of exciting deals with the newspapers. Boy, are we gonna clean up a packet!" And J.C.B. rubbed his hands in glee.

Meanwhile at the motorway works, Boot had discovered the caravan which served as an office for the planning department of the construction company. Maps were pinned all over the walls and spread on the table. Boot took a long careful look at them.

A couple of men in donkey jackets and workmen's helmets were leaning over the table, studying one of the plans. "Straight up through Badger's Wood, that's the route," said one of them. "Should reach the top with the earth-movers first thing Monday morning. It's all easy going round there, just hedgerows and bushes and stuff. We'll have that cleared in a couple of days."

"Haven't you seen the new schedule?" said the other. "We're on to night working as well from tonight. This millionaire bloke Crawley has made a deal with the company – if we can finish the stretch into Wibberley by the end of the month, the company gets a big bonus. So it's on to twenty-four hour working from now on."

"Suits me," said the first man, thinking of the extra money he would earn. "We'll check all the markers after lunch, then we can make a start on the Badger's Wood stretch this afternoon. Pity to see a nice bit of woodland like that disappear, but it's progress, innit?"

"Yup," said the other man, and they went off to lunch.

While they were away, Boot got to work. He

133

found india rubbers and pots of whitener, and he carefully removed the lines on the map which showed the motorway going straight through Badger's Wood. Then he began to draw new lines for the road.

When the men got back from lunch, they picked up the map and went outside. "Let's get those markers checked," said one of them. They walked towards the first marker.

"Hold on a minute," said one of them. "Something funny here. This ain't the same map. Leastways it's been changed."

The other one peered at it. "You're right," he said. "But look. That explains it."

The first man read out what was now written in the corner of the map. "CHANGE OF PLAN. New root for motorway by order of Mr Crawley."

"New root?" queried the first man. "Someone can't spell." (Spelling was not Boot's strong point.)

"And it's a funny-looking route, this one," said his colleague. "It goes slap through the middle of this here castle."

"Oh well," said the other man, "like we said, it's progress, innit?"

22

Live From Wibberley

After a comfortable night at the castle, Wellington had cheered up a bit, deciding that he and Boot might as well co-operate with J.C.B., at least for the live television preview which was scheduled for that evening.

This preview, which would be seen by viewers all around the world, and for which J.C.B. would receive enormous amounts of money, would consist of part of the ghosts' show *Spookeasy*. It would be an advertisement for the show itself, which would open at the theatre as soon as the motorway was finished.

"We must give of our best, laddie," Wellington told Boot. "After all, there will be millions watching us, *millions*, laddie, thanks to that marvellous invention. We mustn't let the old profession down. We actors must give of our best."

Boot nodded, but not very enthusiastically. After his brief expedition to the motorway workings, he had turned up at the castle and had behaved very quietly. But unlike Wellington, he hadn't had a good night's sleep. All those years of sleeping under the bed rather than in it had accustomed him to hard floors, and he wasn't comfortable on the ultra-de-luxe mattress in the bedroom that had been given him.

At five o'clock that evening both the white Rollses, JCB 1 and JCB 2, left the castle for the Theatre Royal. The first car was driven by J.C.B. himself, and Wellington and Boot rode in the back. As it turned out of the castle gates, J.C.B. noticed that the motorway works seemed to have come very close to the wall of the castle grounds. He had been told that the new road would stay at least half a mile away from his land. He made a mental note to raise hell with the planners in the morning. But there wasn't time now.

Just as the second Rolls, JCB 2, turned out of the gate, Krystle, who was sitting in the back with Cherie, saw one of the bulldozers begin to knock down the wall. "Mum, look!" she said. "The motorway people are smashing into our garden!"

"Must be some new idea of yer dad's," said Cherie, who was busy admiring the sheen on her newly-waxed legs, as the chauffeur drove silently on.

It was almost impossible to drive up to the theatre because of the crowds. Faces were pressed to the windows of both Rollses as people tried to get a glimpse of the Wibberley ghosts. In fact both Wellington and Boot, obeying instructions from J.C.B., had dematerialised as their car reached the outskirts of the town. "Remember, boys," J.C.B. told them, "don't let the punters see anything free of charge. They gotta pay for it."

At the theatre it was even more chaotic than the day before, except that the workmen had disappeared and been replaced by television crews. Everywhere there were people with cameras, lights, microphones, and cables. Young women with clipboards and headphones rushed to and fro shouting orders, and everyone seemed to be bossing everyone else. In the middle of all this, the audience was arriving.

The mayor of Wibberley, Councillor Mrs Scroggs, was there in her chain of office and her hat with the artificial fruit. But she was entirely put in the shade by several duchesses in furs and jewels, two or three famous pop singers, and a whole horde of rich businessmen and their wives, each more overdressed than the other. Everywhere, press photographers' cameras kept flashing.

Wellington and Boot disappeared backstage to look for their dressing rooms. "Sorry, love, I don't have your names on the list," said a girl who wore a badge saying "Stage Manager".

Wellington looked at her unbelievingly. "But we," he said grandly, "are the stars of the show."

"Not according to my list you're not. Anyway, all the dressing rooms are taken. Quite apart from the staff allocation, there's the dancers, the comic, and the magician and his assistants."

"Dancers?" echoed Wellington unbelievingly. "Comic? Magician?"

"That's right," said the girl. "There's a whole hour of other acts before they let the Wibberley ghosts come on."

"I see," said Wellington, his hurt pride a little mended by the recollection that, in the days of Victorian music hall, the most important performers had always come on last. "In that case," he told the stage manager, "we will watch the other acts from the wings."

"Not allowed," said the stage manager. "Only TV crews allowed in the wings. If you want to see the show, I suppose you can pop down to the basement. There's a TV set there you can see it on."

Wellington looked at Boot. The two of them shrugged their shoulders, and went down the stairs.

They could scarcely see the TV set, because about a dozen men and women in shirt sleeves, who seemed to have nothing to do but drink coke out of tins, were hanging about watching it too. Nobody paid any attention to the ghosts.

After a while the endless advertisements that had been showing gave way to the logo of the TV company, and a voice said, "And now, a very special presentation. Live from Wibberley-on-the-Wold, it's . . . *Spookeasy*."

Up in the theatre, Krystle was sitting with J.C.B. and Cherie in the royal box. The whole place was looking magnificent – the new gold paint and red velvet curtains were glowing wonderfully in the television lights.

The invitations had been sent out by J.C.B.'s personal assistant's personal assistant's assistant, who only ever wrote letters to the rich and famous, or the rich and gullible; and since the Murrays weren't the slightest bit rich or famous or important, they weren't on the list of the personal assistant's personal assistant's assistant.

Everyone at 17 Cherrytree Close felt the slight very badly.

"Might as well pretend we're there, mightn't we, Morris?" said Muriel, switching on their old telly, and hoping it wasn't on the blink as usual. Morris, sitting on a bean-bag, nodded glumly. Muriel had come up with several ways to punish him for the loss of "their" Theatre Royal. Banishing him from the family settee to a bean-bag was one of them.

The screen flickered uncertainly into black-and-white life. Muriel caught a glimpse of some all-too-familiar faces in the royal box, a bottle of champagne at J.C.B.'s elbow.

"And to think that it could've been *us*, Morris," moaned Muriel, reaching for a bottle of cheap tonic wine. "*Us*, Morris, up in the royal box at the opening of *our* theatre." Morris said nothing, but shifted miserably on his bean-bag.

"Just be quiet, Mum, and watch," said Keith.

From the TV set came a roll of drums and a fanfare of brass. The houselights went down, and a famous comedian stepped through the curtain and waved. The audience responded with a great cheer and much clapping.

"What do they want *him* in the show for?" said Keith scornfully.

"Well, hello everybody!" said the comic, grinning into the TV cameras. "Aren't you going to say hello back to me, don't you *spook* when you're *spooken* to?"

There were roars of laughter at this. In the royal box, Krystle murmured, "Whata loada rubbish. Geddim off."

"Shush, Princess," said J.C.B., patting her on the arm. "Costa loada money, he did."

The comic was continuing with his patter. "You know who we got to write the gags for this spooky show tonight, folks? Not script writers, but *crypt writers*!!!" The audience went wild at this one.

"That's a good one," said Morris Murray, watching the show at home. "*Crypt* writers. Get it, Keithie?"

"Yes, Dad," said Keith.

Down in the basement of the theatre, Wellington and Boot got it too. How could the man get away with such rubbish? They looked at each other, and then, without being noticed by the other people who were clustered around the TV set, they both dematerialised.

The comic was finishing his act. "Mine's a really clean act," he told the audience. "I've had it cleaned up by some really special cleaners. They're ghosts who do cleaning as a sideline. And do you know what they call themselves? *Ghostdusters*! Goodnight, folks!"

And to roars of laughter, cheers, and huge applause, he began to walk off the stage.

Halfway across, he tripped and fell flat on his face.

At this, the audience laughed even more, because they assumed he'd done it on purpose. In fact, something invisible had tripped him up. And he was very cross indeed.

He got to his feet, stumbled off the stage, and swore at the stage manager. "What are your lot doing, leaving cables all over the place? I might have broken my neck."

"I can't see any cables, love," said the stage manager. And indeed there weren't any cables where the comic had tripped.

Now the music was striking up again, and the curtain rose to reveal a row of dancers, dressed in costumes decorated with little green ghosts. They opened their mouths, and on the loudspeakers, a song began. It had been written especially for the occasion by that famous songwriter Andrew Floyd-Rubber. It was called "Be My Ghost".

I've got that haunting feeling,

it began,

You're always sending shivers up and down my spine.
Baby, you say you've seen right through me,
So don't lose your head, but run to me,
The spectre of your leaving me don't make me feel fine,
So baby, Be my ghost! Yeah!

"Clever stuff, these modern songwriters turn out," said Morris. "None of your corny old moon, June, spoon stuff."

"Usual Floyd-Rubber rubbish," said Keith.

"And dreadful dancing," squeaked Muriel. "Just think what I could've done, Morris, given half a chance . . ."

In the wings, Wellington and Boot, both invisible, were watching the dancers.

"Have you noticed something?" Wellington whispered to Boot. "Those young ladies *aren't actually singing*. They're opening and shutting their mouths, but the sounds are all proceeding from those boxes on the wall."

It was perfectly true. The dancers were miming to a prerecorded tape.

Boot left the wings and made his way to the control box where the tape was operated. Just as he did so, the orchestra on the prerecorded tape changed key, and the dancers prepared to launch into the final verse of "Be My Ghost".

But suddenly the loudspeakers went dead. There was a slight pause, and then a distant wind-up gramophone could be heard playing "Tea for Two".

Boot had switched off the tape machine, and Wellington had spotted their old wind-up gramophone in a corner of the wings, and had put the record on.

For a few seconds the dancers went on opening and shutting their mouths, but they looked very silly, and after a moment they all ran off the stage in confusion. There was another pause, and then jerkily the curtain came down.

The comic hurried on to the stage again. "Sorry about that, everyone, just a slight technical hitch. But I can assure you that nothing ever goes wrong when our next star makes his appearance. Yes, ladies and gentlemen, I'm talking about that master of TV magic . . . Willy the Wizard!"

At this point there was supposed to be another recorded fanfare from the loudspeakers, but the tape operator was still struggling to discover what was wrong with his equipment. So there was no music, and the audience, still puzzled by the abrupt ending of the dancers' act, only applauded rather half-heartedly.

"This better be good," muttered J.C.B. in the royal box. "Oh boy, this better be flamin' good."

The curtain rose, but then it got stuck and seemed to come down again. The audience started to laugh. J.C.B. swore.

"What's up?" said Keith, watching at home.

Krystle, in the royal box, bit her lip and tried not to laugh. She could guess what was up.

Sure enough, backstage, an invisible Boot had managed to get himself tangled in the ropes that worked the curtain, so that it wouldn't go up properly. On stage, Willy the Wizard, a fat little man in a spotted bow tie, was swearing at the stage manager and telling her to get the curtain up fast, or he'd walk out.

Boot disentangled himself, and the curtain rose while Willy was still shouting at the stage manager. He looked round and discovered that everyone was watching him. The audience laughed at this, and J.C.B. began to bite his nails.

"Hello, ladies and gentlemen, boys and girls," said Willy the Wizard, trying to look cheerful. "Tonight we've got a really magical trick for you. You've heard of sawing the lady in half? Well, I'm going to saw *two* ladies in half. So give a big hand, please, to my lovely assistants, Tracy and Samantha."

The sound operator, who had managed to get his tape machine working again, put on a fanfare, and the audience started to applaud. But nobody walked on to the stage. Where were Tracy and Samantha?

In fact Tracy and Samantha had just been locked into their dressing room by Boot, who had also stolen one of their dresses. He materialised, put on the dress, and also put on the old yellow wig he had worn as Cinderella, which he had kept in his pocket ever since. Dressed like this, he walked on to the stage.

The audience roared with laughter, but Willy the Wizard didn't think it was funny at all. "Who the hell are you?" he hissed at Boot. "Get off at once."

Boot grinned at him.

"Who the hell is that?" muttered J.C.B. Sitting next to him, Krystle smiled. If her dad didn't recognise one of his own ghosts, that was *his* problem.

Back at Cherrytree Close, Keith recognised Boot all right. "We should have some fun now," he said.

23

Grand Finale

Having failed to get Boot off the stage and get Tracy and Samantha on, Willy the Wizard smiled glassily at the audience and the TV cameras.

"It looks like I'm sawing just one girl into half tonight," he gagged. Then he turned and muttered at Boot, "If you don't do as I tell you, you flaming well *will* get sawn in half. Into the box, and do as I say."

Grinning happily back at Willy the Wizard, Boot climbed into the magician's box.

Willy the Wizard picked up his saw, while from the loudspeakers there came a roll of drums. He flourished the saw at the audience and the cameras, then fitted it to a groove in the box. "Get into the secret compartment at the back," he hissed to Boot inside the box. "Pull the little handle, and it'll open up."

Willy the Wizard passed the saw through the box, and out the other side. "There you are, ladies and gentlemen, boys and girls," he announced with a broad smile. "There's no way any living human being could have stayed in one piece inside that box. But look!" And he opened the box.

What the audience expected to see was Boot still in one piece. What they actually saw was Boot in *two* pieces. He had ignored Willy the Wizard's instructions, and had stayed exactly where he was inside the box. Being a ghost, the saw hadn't hurt him in the least. After all, it was no different from coming apart like he so often did.

So when Willy the Wizard opened the box, Boot climbed out in two pieces. His bottom half walked off the stage in one direction. His top half floated off the stage in the other. And Willy the Wizard turned white as a sheet and fainted.

The curtain came down again, and there was a buzz of astonishment among the audience. What on earth was going on?

"What is flaming going on?" asked J.C.B. in the royal box.

"Whaddya *think's* going on, Dad?" said Krystle. "You've got two ghosts back there, who are bored to tears with being pushed around and kept hanging about. They're just havin' a good time and getting up to some funny pranks, that's all."

"Well, they can keep their flamin' pranks," raged J.C.B. "I didn't hire them to be funny. I hired them to be *ghosts*." And he stormed out of the royal box to see what was going on backstage. Krystle looked at her programme. It said "Grand finale: the Wibberley ghosts."

Backstage, everything was in complete chaos. Wellington was nowhere to be seen. Boot was visible one moment, invisible the next. He seemed to be clambering about among the ropes above the stage, judging by the pieces of scenery that kept flying

146

up and down, making it dangerous for anyone to walk around. He was also interfering with the sound and lighting; the strangest noises and oddest lighting effects kept happening. The audience was getting very restive.

"*Where are those flaming ghosts*?" yelled J.C.B., arriving backstage. "Tell them to get on stage and do their stuff, or I'll . . . I'll *kill* them."

"Not much good killing a ghost, Mr Crawley," said a voice. It was Herring, the chief accountant of Crawleyhomes, who was looking very worried. "The TV people are going to abandon the programme unless you can get things right straightaway, Mr Crawley," he warned J.C.B. "And that means we lose . . . *millions*."

J.C.B. turned to the quaking stage manager. "Where are those flamin' ghosts?" he yelled.

"No idea, Mr Crawley."

J.C.B. turned to Herring. "Don't just stand there like a flamin' fish outa water, Herring – get one of these things on." He threw Herring an old dust sheet that was lying in the wings, and found one for himself. "Okay, you!" he boomed at the terrified stage manager. "Cue sound and flamin' lights!"

The lights dimmed, and there came a loud roll from the drums. "And *now*," said a deep voice on the loudspeakers. "The moment you've *all* been *waiting for*! Ladies and gentlemen, for the first time, live in this theatre and on your television screens . . . we present the world-famous WIBBERLEY GHOSTS!"

The curtain rose.

"This should be interesting," said a quiet voice next to Krystle, from J.C.B.'s seat. She turned.

"Hey!" she gasped. It was Wellington. "But if

147

you're up here . . . then who's down there?"

"Exactly, dear child," said Wellington. "Well, we shall see."

The curtain rose in darkness, and beyond it, two white shapes were swirling up and down. The audience, impressed, gave a gasp. At home, Keith said: "But that's not them. They don't go around in old sheets."

"They're giving the public what it wants, son," said Morris. "Old troupers like them know that when Joe Public hears the word 'ghosts', he thinks of spooks in white sheets."

"Don't talk rubbish, Dad, it's *not them*." And a moment later Keith was proved right.

Something invisible – guess who – tripped up the two "ghosts" and pulled their dust-sheets aside to reveal J.C.B. and Mr Herring. They blinked, stared at the audience and the cameras, and ran off the stage.

The audience went wild. "Cheats!" they shouted. "Cheats! Cheats! Cheats! We want our money back! *We want our money back!*"

Backstage, J.C.B. sank down exhausted. "Herring," he said, "we gotta give them their money back."

"Yes, Mr Crawley."

"And we gotta give the TV people their money back, Herring."

"Yes, Mr Crawley."

"And we gotta give all them Americans and Japanese and all those thousands of people who've booked to fly to England to see the Wibberley ghosts, we gotta give them all their money back."

"Yes, Mr Crawley."

"This is going to cost us millions, Herring."

"Yes, Mr Crawley."

"Millions and millions and millions."

"Yes, Mr Crawley."

"How'm I gonna raise all those millions, Herring?"

Mr Herring thought for a few moments. "You could sell Crawley Castle, Mr Crawley."

J.C.B. nodded. "I'm gonna do that, Herring. I'm gonna sell Crawley Castle, an' with all the millions I'll raise from that, I'll pay 'em all back, and Crawleyhomes will just about keep afloat. Good thinkin', Herring."

"Thank you, Mr Crawley."

But when they all got back to Crawley Castle it had vanished. There was just an enormous mess of stones and mud, and a big sign saying "Motorway under construction".

24

Business as Usual

"Special gala edition!" shouted the voice of the newspaper seller outside the Theatre Royal, Wibberley-on-the-Wold. "Special gala edition of the *Woldshire Chronicle*." On the poster, it said: "Special edition to celebrate REOPENING OF THE THEATRE ROYAL."

On the wall of the theatre another poster said:

For Two Weeks Only
Commencing Wednesday 26th December 1990
The THEATRE ROYAL, Wibberley-on-the-Wold
(Proprietor: T. Scroggs, Gen. Manager: M. Murray)
Proudly presents
BABES IN THE WOOD
A Traditional Pantomime
Featuring the Muriel du Maurier Dancers
BOOK EARLY TO AVOID DISAPPOINTMENT

"Special gala edition!" repeated the newspaper seller, and Morris Murray, arriving for work at the theatre, bought a paper from him. "Keep the change," he said, giving the man fifty pence.

J.C.B. Crawley pocketed the ten pence change, and thanked Morris politely. Ten pence wasn't much, but if he was going to build up his financial empire again from scratch, every little bit counted.

Morris walked breezily in through the main entrance of the theatre. "Morning, Mrs C.," he called to the usherette, who was getting the programmes and ice-creams ready to sell at the first performance that afternoon.

"Morning, Mr Murray," said Cherie Crawley, adjusting her new usherette's cap.

Old Mr Scroggs, whom the lawyers sorting out the collapse of Crawleyhomes had judged to be the rightful owner of the theatre, had called in to check that Morris could cope on what would certainly be a busy day – there was the box office to run as well as everything else. "Nice to see the place running normally again," he said to Morris. "Business as usual, eh? Just like it used to be."

"Right you are," said Morris. "Mind you, I still say those gnomes would've made my fortune in the end. It was just a matter of time."

On stage, Muriel was taking her dancers for a last run-through of the finale. "One – two – three – and kick," she called, while in the orchestra pit the pianist, drummer, and other musicians banged away happily. "And sing out, everyone! We don't have any miming here!"

When the rehearsal was finished, Keith said to Krystle, "You look a bit nervous."

"Well, we have got the main parts, you and me, and the curtain goes up in a couple of hours. Shall we go out and look at the shops?"

It was fun shopping in Wibberley now. The Crawley Centre had lost most of its customers after Wellington and Boot had gone on the rampage there, and with the collapse of Crawleyhomes it had closed down. The Wibberley Town Council was knocking it down, and had decided to bring back the old cattle-market, so that farmers could buy and sell animals locally, instead of having to drive them miles and miles in lorries.

And on the subject of lorries, Boot's diversion of the motorway through the grounds of Crawley Castle meant that the traffic from Birmingham wouldn't be coming into Wibberley at all. In fact the motorway, which was now open, avoided the town entirely and veered off to the north. Since it ran in completely the wrong direction, nobody used it, and there was talk of closing it and returning the land to fields and woods.

Meanwhile in Wibberley, the new hotels that had been begun when all the tourists were expected on account of the Wibberley ghosts, had now been abandoned. They and all the unsold Crawleyhomes were being cleared away, and the council was planning a new park.

Inspired by all these changes, the Crawley Executive Motor Lodge had knocked down its shoddy modern extensions and had reverted to calling itself the Pied Bull.

The town was becoming very pleasant again.

"On second thoughts, let's not go out there now," said Krystle. "Let's go up and see *them*."

Keith knew very well who she meant. But, strangely enough, everyone seemed to have forgotten about the ghosts, or to have decided that they'd probably never existed – which, given the chaos on the night of the TV show, wasn't very surprising. And Keith and Krystle had managed to restore the wardrobe to roughly what it had looked like before. The room was kept locked, and only they had a key.

"The kids have got some stuff upstairs they play with," Morris explained to Mr Scroggs. "Keeps 'em happy for hours. Just old costumes and the like."

"Oh yes?" said Mr Scroggs, who had a private opinion that much more than costumes could be found behind that locked door. But he kept his notions to himself.

Krystle knocked on the door, and when Wellington called "Come in!", she unlocked it and turned the handle.

The ghosts were sitting happily in front of the window, watching all the comings and goings. "So nice to see the old place being used properly," said Wellington. "I hope you aren't nervous, my dears?"

"Yes," said Keith, "I'm afraid we are."

Wellington laughed. "That's the stuff, laddie. A true actor is *always* nervous. But go on and give them all you've got! And we'll be there, though you won't see us. We'll be watching in the wings."

"Are you sure you don't want to do some more acting yourselves?" asked Krystle. "Isn't it boring, just sitting here while all the fun is going on in the theatre?"

"Not a bit of it," said Wellington, and Boot shook his head in agreement. "Thanks to you, we've had a very exciting time. And who knows, there may be more exciting times ahead. But just for the moment my friend and I feel that we need a little rest." And

Boot nodded. "After all," Wellington continued, "we are both about a hundred and fifty years old, and we think it's time the younger generation did some of the theatrical hard work. Now, don't forget, both of you, speak your lines clearly, just as we've taught you. Speak up, act out, and you'll be the stars of the show. Won't they, Boot?" said Wellington.

And Boot nodded.

Humphrey Carpenter
Charlie Crazee's Teevee £2.99

Have you ever thought how boring a lot of the programmes on TV
are?

How about setting up your own TV station using your neighbours to
help out?

That's exactly how Charlie's Crazee Teevee comes about – all you
need is a granny with a kitchen, a few friends and an eccentric
do-it-all boff for some great TV and hilarious adventures.

Dick Cate
Alexander and the Tooth of Zaza £2.99

'Keep calm everyone, *please*! Shut up and stop shouting! Now . . .
everybody move into the dining room for trifle! Move!'

If there's anything worse than a birthday party you don't want to go
to, it's being ordered around when you get there!

All Alexander could do was wait for the moment when he could
swipe the largest cherry trifle from right under Eric Polecat's nose.
Then things started to happen. In came the Nagasaki Knee-Jerk . . .

. . . and out came Zaza's tooth!